My Body is my Business

Melissa Todd

Clink Street

Published by Clink Street Publishing 2021

Copyright © 2021

First edition.

ISBN:
978-1-914498-13-8 - paperback
978-1-914498-14-5 - ebook

For my mum

Chapter One

"There's been a lot less rape than I was led to expect."

Philip groaned, and arched his back against the cushions, thrusting his bottom out for the cane. I administered three blistering stingers, quicker than heartbeats, leaving him not a moment to breathe or recover. He bit down hard on his thumb, hard enough to leave teeth marks, then pushed his buttocks skyward once more.

"I mean, growing up, it was all, don't go there, don't wear that, you'll be raped, nonstop rape opportunities. And I went on a march at uni to 'reclaim the night' – can't say for sure whether we got it or not, didn't matter, the inference was clear; we were reclaiming the night from the rapists, of whom there were millions. Now it's all you see on Facebook, women posting endless memes, ten a day some of them, about how awful rape is, how men can't possibly understand what a terrifying, hideous violation rape constitutes… you must have seen them?"

"Well, I don't really do social media, so…"

"Very wise. Dreadful waste of time." I found a stingier beast discarded on the sofa and whipped it on to the upper part of his thighs, tutting at his squeals. "Neighbours, Philip! I'm meant to be doing your accounts, remember? 'Ooh, just imagine it, though, really think about it, hard, being taken against your will by a biker gang, one after the other, having them watch and egg each other on, deep in a wood where no one could hear you scream–' yeah alright, Nicola, we get it, Alan isn't exciting you quite as much as the early days, poor fella. Try not to make it so damn obvious, eh? Are you ready for the stirrup whip?"

"You're in charge."

"Oh that's right. Well, I say you are." I picked up a homemade creation, two stirrups attached to a paintbrush handle, soaked in oil, heavy and deadly. I had to stand well back for this one. It left some beautiful bruising. Worse than the cane, in many ways. The pain is intense with a cane, but fades fast; those thick lumps of leather leave great thuddy welts that take weeks to vanish. Especially on Philip, who takes Warfarin and bruises at a handshake.

"I've never been raped. They'd struggle with me, mind. I'll have to gag you if you keep making that row. Here…" I pushed a leather slipper into his mouth, stood back and administered a great, glorious thwack, vicious enough to make the chandelier rattle. "Not that I'm a karate expert, you understand; I'm just perpetually willing. 'Ooh, unexpected cock, smashing, where would you like me?' Most of the men I've known have been scared, prissy creatures, frightened to put a finger wrong in case I rise up against them in full female fury and ruin their careers in consequence. Even outside of work. You're starting to bleed a bit, even with the plasters. I think we'd better stop. Sorry. Probably the bath brush did for you."

He spat out the slipper and stood up. I handed him a paper towel to mop himself down and spare the carpet. Philip has a soft hairy belly that makes me ache to touch it, and prominent brown nipples he likes twisted and smacked. Bottom broken beyond repair, I dug my nails nipple-wards instead.

"Aaaggh! You're complaining about the lack of rape? Really?"

"Not exactly. I'm just saying a ludicrously disproportionate amount of time is given over to worrying about it. When there are so many worse things that could happen to a woman, and vastly more likely to boot. Like poverty. Where are your pants? Please tell me you came in dark trousers this time. Can't have the blood dribbling all down your thighs at the station, can we? Not again. Here, I'll tuck some kitchen roll round your cheeks. Have you got everything?" I looked round, ostensibly being mother, actually checking he'd left my fee. Clocked it on the dresser, a thick fold of notes that a good girl might expect to receive in return for 40 hours tedious, mind-numbing graft. He liked to leave it discreetly, the better to pretend this was a social engagement with a slightly dotty chum, rather than a professional transaction. And I liked Philip hugely and was perfect happy to indulge this notion. We read the same books, voted the same way, recommended plays and art exhibitions to one another over cups of tea in my kitchen, before I lead him to the punishment room and thrashed the skin off him, then sent him home to his wife.

I had a husband recently. Of my own, I mean, for a change. Not for long. He took off, the way they tend to. He didn't like my job. Tried to deal with it, not very hard, failed, fucked off. Made it sound like my fault. But I've never hidden what I am. It's out there in my outfit, my belligerence, and I like to talk about it, it's fun. I like making the straitlaced wonder a bit.

Bleeding having stopped play, I'd half an hour to kill before the next one. Philip scuttled off, talking rather loudly about how I was the best thrasher in the biz and how he could get his bum in training for our next session, despite my agonised glances at the neighbours. So. Pub. Laptop to answer emails, but chiefly pub. The next punter lived in a gated community five miles away, irritatingly close to Paul and Samantha, vanilla chums who would want to give me tea and demand an explanation if they saw me near their home. I needed a wee stiffener. Also, Bernie likes to be pissed on, so I could probably offset the pint against tax. I checked my hair and lipstick, powdered my tell-tale shiny forehead, smooth and white as a skating rink, then ducked past the neighbours – perfectly lovely, many children, can't remember any of their damn names, always smiled, took in parcels, but you don't want to take chances, not when you commit GBH professionally from home all day long – and got in my car, an unremarkable Ford Focus. I could have a Porsche, but that would draw attention. As far as they all know, I'm an accountant.

Shit pub, barn-large echoing corporate swirly carpeted noisy slot machine monstrosity, but it's handy, the beer's cheap and the wifi's not too temperamental. It will even let you get on Onlyfans. So it should. Tame as they come, Onlyfans. You'd assume it's all tits and gash, but trust me, you won't get far on there if that's all you're offering. Tits and gash are everywhere, gratis. They want a slice of the real you, or the real you you're pretending to be. I arranged my pint of Guinness for a picture, wincing a little at the knowledge the chap on the next table saw me do it, doubtless thought I was some Instagram wannabe twat, posting pretty pictures free, screw that; uploaded it, after a moment's thought, with the caption – "Richly deserved break in my hectic day. One lucky chap will be enjoying some flavoursome mistress champagne soon!" Bugger it, that'll do. Emails.

Can I do a school day on the 13th? I can. Do you see ladies? I do, although no lady I've ever seen has ever referred to herself as a lady, and you are a trannie. Can you punish my girlfriend while I watch? I could, although this is clearly wank fodder and I doubt you've ever had a girlfriend. Next table chap is typing too. His machine is bigger than mine, and he's more pint left. We look like mummy and daddy bear, and our typing falls into a pleasing syncopation. This pub is the closest I get to office camaraderie. He's scowling and jabbing at keys like a toddler, looks up, sees me staring.

"Wifi keeps dropping."

"It's shit in that corner. Come more into the middle. There." I extended a long red fingernail towards another table, briefly hypnotised by my own shiny perfection.

"But the plug's here."

"Yeah. It's like they don't want you to hang out here for hours working. You can sit here if you like. I'm going soon." I indicated the double plug at my black patent heel. Look this isn't Fifty Shades, I'm not going to waste hours telling you about my Louboutins and fully fashioned seamed silk hosiery. The shoes were from New Look, fair enough, but shiny and pointy and plenty good enough for this dump. New Look do excellent slut shoes, there, top tip, gratis. He didn't even seem to notice.

"You've got the prime spot, clearly."

"Of course." I watched his hand flashing white beside my stocking. Large manly sort of hand, no ring, blue veins stark against the white. It grazed against my ankle.

"Sorry!"

"S'alright."

He didn't even look at me. Went back to tapping. Side by side now. I could smell him, musky, slightly metallic, very clean. His hair a sort of blond white mop. He could almost be albino. Good posture. No, you can't spank me, Barry, because we tried that and you wouldn't behave. And no I don't want to spank you for being such a naughty boy last time, because what the hell sort of punishment would that be, given you're actually paying me to do it, you lemon?

We'd fallen into a rhythmic glug and tap pattern of which he seemed to be unconscious. I tried yawning to see if he would copy me. He didn't. So I, then, was aping his body language. Something about his total indifference to me felt rare enough to be intriguing. I sucked in my belly, sat up straight, stuck my tits out, twirled a curl round a finger. Nothing.

Ian wanted to be hit with a wooden Scholl sandal – picture please – and also wondered if I offered medical role-play, which, if I twatted him with that bastard, he'd probably need for real. I did have wooden Scholl sandals actually. Donald had bought me a pair. He liked me to slip off my heels and thrust my sweaty toes into those clumpy clogs and walk up and down a few times, thud thud slap, the way nanny used to, before taking my belt to him. I encourage the fetishes that mean I can work in comfort. Tights, jeans, jodhpurs, slippers, all excellent. Could I let him know when I next visit Milton Keynes? I promised faithfully I would, knowing I'd forget the second I pressed send. Khalid wanted me to visit Dubai. Well, I wouldn't mind that, if it were real. I had seen him before. Hotel at Heathrow. He'd paid me for a three-hour session and slept away three-quarters of it. We'd drawn some glances in the bar after, me twice his height., tipsy, radiantly Western against his firm Arab arm. Spot the whore.

In unison we drained our pints. I slammed mine down on the table, ostentatious. Gazes locked. There was a slight smile, maybe shy, maybe indifferent.

"I'm getting another."

"I've got to go to work."

"Yeah, you said. Could you just watch my stuff for me? I won't be a minute."

The unbelievable rude shit.

"Of course."

"Cheers." And he skipped off without another glance. I considered walking off, obviously. Instead I admired his arse, which was prominent, faintly gorilla-like, telling of Sunday mornings spent running round parks; then glanced at the screen he'd been fool enough to leave open. He was writing a lengthy document about Venezuelan refugees, of whom he appeared to be broadly in favour. Some sort of do-gooder. Probably hated sluts. Ostentatiously I busied myself with packing my guff as he walked back. Phone, laptop, chargers, a kilo of makeup. A slightly mucky tissue fell on to the table. I snatched at it, hating myself for blushing. He sat down. "Thanks."

"Excused now, am I?"

"You are excused."

For a long moment we looked at each other in silence. He had that unbearable public school confidence of someone who knew no one could really ever be seriously cross with him, no, nor that things could ever go truly, badly wrong; the confidence of old money and a certain future, mingled with twinkly eyes, obscenely blue, like marbles. I had an urge to fuck him up, but couldn't think how. Instead I gave a deep bow and strode to the door, looking back to see if he'd seen the extra wiggle he'd given my walk. He was already immersed in his refugees. It's frankly obscene to have so much time and energy spare you lavish it on strangers. Strangers who can't even pay. What's he trying to escape?

Bernie, now, trying to escape loneliness so vivid it bordered on insanity, impending death, a wretched job and indifferent family – this I could conquer. I stepped into his lounge, a long narrow room with large windows overlooking the Thames. We could watch people punting past, should we choose. I closed the curtains. Then rummaged under make up, laptop, chargers, for his heart's delight, all while he watched, perched on the corner of his sofa, like a puppy trembling at an impending scolding. At last I produced yesterday's pants and pushed them over his head. Then pushed him over the sofa to start caning him, methodically, silently. He squirmed and twisted his buttocks to make the process trickier, like shooting a moving duck at a fairground. Well. His ass. After I'd caught him on the kidneys a few times and hissed at him to keep still, slapping his face to reinforce the message, he did as he was told. After five minutes of that he removed the pants, hugged me tenderly and went to the fridge for champagne.

"Been busy, have you?"

"Extremely. Everyone wants me. How are your girlfriends?" An old tired joke based on the existence of two widows, who let him take them out to dinner so they could drink expensive wine in quantity and cry about their husbands.

"Oh, you know, going nowhere. And you…?"

I forestalled the question by topping up my glass and taking my skirt off. "Now, the sight of my thighs demands a – twelve stroke penalty I think? And if you want the blouse off too, another twelve. Same for bra. Twenty-four for pants, and if you want to suck my toes…" He assumed the position, pants over nose. I beat him and make him enunciate clearly, "Please, Mistress, may I have another?", and when he failed to be sufficiently articulate, I took my belt to him. I am accurate and hard, possessed of powerful arms and years of experience. He whimpered and squirmed and I slapped his face. Not sure he actually likes the pain, although he's been seeing me years to get it. He pays for the pants in the mouth, really: the beating is largely incidental. Probably he wants to be punished for his fetish, on some level. Whatever. When the knickers are in situ he can hardly see my face or feel my belt, I suspect: only the knickers have any presence or meaning. He likes everything that might fall out of my lower half and get entangled in a knicker, spends his working hours sitting by the women's loos, fantasising about what they must do in there, wiping, pulling up tights; he times each visit and ponders what each must have involved in consequence. This is the kind of behaviour that earns men the label of pervert and makes women avoid them, which seems a shame: it's a fairly harmless hobby, and he can't help it, nor understand it. He doesn't want to shag girls; he wants to know how their pee tastes. Does it harm anyone, I ask you?

I got a pal along to help once. We blindfolded Bernie and had him work out whose pee was whose. He loved that. The Romans tasted pee to diagnose diseases. Quite sensible really. It was Bernie first told me I was pregnant. That's how long I've known him. Beth is 19 now, all curves, sighs and eye-rolls. I drink more until I feel my bladder start to groan, and Bernie's unasked question stops making my skin itch.

Men, however liberated, always want to stop me doing what I want to do. I want to have as many adventures and do as much damage as possible, so no one ever bloody forgets I was here, and of course they all start by claiming they want that too. They simply adore my jolly anecdotes and ravenous sexual appetite, then a few months in start whining that I don't prioritise us, we need to talk more, spend more time together, which fast translates as, please sit on the sofa feeling your hips spread to melted lard while I pretend I'm not looking at porn and messaging someone else. They need the fantasy to stay fantasy, even more than I do. Still, I like feeling them bend to my will for a month or two.

The champagne poured liberally on top of the earlier Guinness was working its way through wonderfully. I slapped Bernie's backside and pointed; he stumbled towards his bathroom, where he lay in the bath, mouth open. He's a short, chubby creature, white haired, broken-veined, a sort of tipsy jolly Santa's elf, and I suspect one day soon he'll be too infirm to climb into his bath, or rather, climb out again, and then his life will effectively be over. Mind you, I wasn't feeling too athletic myself, hauling myself up to squat over his face. Even if you're tipsy and bursting to go, having a man inches from your crotch with his mouth gaping open, fillings and cracked tongue exposed, tends to render your bladder shy. He started tickling my thighs to encourage the flow. He always tried this, and it never helped. I pushed my toes up against his nose to stop him. That did work, oddly. Human bodies are curious beasts. I let rip. Pints of it. Squeezing the pelvic floor every five seconds or so to give him a chance to swallow.

"Mmm! That tastes of – gin?"

"You always guess gin. Guess again." The sour smell hung so heavy in the air I could taste it myself. I wanted to retch. My thighs were soaked.

"Beer!"

"Not specific enough. It was Guinness. So sorry. It'll have to be the sjambok to finish."

I let him hose himself down while I gave myself a cursory lick at his basin, stepping outside to dry my legs. Strange that watching a man shower, dry and dress himself seemed more intimate, more vulgar, than relieving yourself into his mouth. It was the domesticity that disconcerted. I checked my phone while I waited, you're so beautiful I love you when can I see you again I need you you make my life complete. I drained my glass, and after a moment's polite hesitation, his. Started swinging the sjambok when he walked in. He took his place over the sofa and I walloped him hard and fast. The hour was over, thank God. I was sleepy. I had a sudden urge to curl up somewhere against someone warm. I took the wad of cash he'd left under the fruit bowl and left him, my last sight as the door slammed a chap on all fours, chewing peacefully on my pants.

Chapter Two

It had got dark out. Cold too. The wind went right through you, my mum would have said. Stupid gated community wouldn't let me out, so I had to wait for a much nicer car than mine to come in. Idiotic system that conspires to keep the riffraff imprisoned. I drove – yes, probably slightly over the limit, fuck off, this isn't a public information leaflet, I'll behave as I please, you piss on someone sober if you like – back to West Norwood, and the flat I shared with a girl named Katie. Originally a punter, she'd begged me about two years ago to live in her spare room and dispense beatings as rent. Well, I can't resist a bargain and I'd just got myself out of a pickle, so agreed, although it was a shabby little place, miles from civilisation and with no central heating, just a medieval oil burner affair, over which we both had to dry our smalls: the flat smelled permanently of singed nylon. I think she probably regretted the idea now. Not that I beat her constantly, far from it; rather, having had a hard day of it, seldom had I any desire to tell her she'd been a naughty girl and should go to my room and take a brutal flogging then lick me until I was satisfied, as she desperately desired. More usually I wanted to curl up on her sofa and read trashy thrillers. Like I say, keep fantasy as fantasy. It's no fun when it intrudes on real life.

Katie was waiting for me in the kitchen, wine opened, gnocchi simmering. This unnerved me. Usually she drank tea during the week and ignored me. Never did she cook. She must want to be beaten very badly, and my arm ached already.

"Evening Cla! Good day? Been busy, have you?"

No-one calls me Cla. No one. I named myself after a character in an obscure Victorian novel, a good time girl who came to a bad end, which I'll probably come to regret, and quite soon too. I eased off my heels, flexing my toes, and wondered what was going on.

"Oh, you know. Did I not clear up all the blood?"

"What? Oh – yes – no – I haven't seen any." She flushed and reached for her wine. She hates being reminded of the existence of other punters, and more, my casual indifference to them.

"Cool. So what's up?"

"Nothing. Only." Deep breath, more swigging. "I've met someone."

"About time! Fetlife finally throw up an actual human?"

"I met Alex at work. He's not kinky. He's our office manager."

"A he? Gosh. Well. Congratulations, I guess. Maybe you can corrupt him, given time."

"I don't want to corrupt him! It's – different."

Oh. Fuck.

"How long has this been going on?" I said, hating myself for sounding like an aggrieved wife.

"Almost eight months."

"An aeon."

"And now – today – we started talking about his maybe moving in here."

I wondered whether to be outraged, indignant, tearful; plead for mercy, cry, shout. I stared at the table and stalled for time. I could probably guilt her into letting me stay, at least for a bit, until this Alex wanker made life intolerable. Much as I moan about the flat, it's been home for two years and means I can claim London on my Adultwork profile, and so reasonably charge more. All the punters know where I am. There's parking. It's a mere eight-minute walk from the overground, although admittedly hours before it gets you anywhere decent. But maybe I should take this as a sign from the gods and clear off. But where, for Christ's sake? Do you know how hard it is to work from home when you beat people? The noise, the constant stream of traffic to your door? No decent landlord or neighbourhood will stand it. And you try getting a mortgage when you're paid entirely in cash. Maybe a mobile home on Leysdown. Christ.

"I see." I sighed deeply.

"And so we will need the spare room for when his son comes to stay, Clara, and anyway, he'll hate all the bondage gear and gym horse – and, you know, this was only meant to be temporary."

That was definitely today's invention, the lying cow. "But you love the bondage equipment and gym horse. Does he think he can straighten you out?"

"He – I haven't exactly told him all about what I – what I've done."

"Oh Jesus. So you're going to give up your passion, your true self, for an office manager with a kid? I'll tell you what's temporary if you like."

Her breathing quickened. "Oh don't, please! Don't say that. I want a chance to be normal. Have a normal life. I'm 30 next year!"

Ouch. "You poor old crone."

"I want children. Trips to Ikea."

"You told me you found sex abhorrent. You told me you could only come in a nappy over my knee with a vibe, getting whacked–"

"Sssshhh!"

"What, is he here?"

"I hadn't met the right man, that's all. You know we – it hasn't been exactly what I – what we'd hoped – between us –"

An unaccustomed stab of remorse pierced my gut. I should have taken better care of Katie. I should have protected my investments. I thought, having made her mine, I could keep her forever without any further thought. I'd been a bloody idiot, and now I was a homeless one. She got up to stir the stupid gnocchi.

"I'm not hungry."

"Oh please – you must eat – don't be like this! I want us to be friends. All of us."

All of us. For crying out loud. I reached for her hand, stiff and cold as a dead bird, greasy from her conciliatory cooking efforts. I still couldn't decide whether being outraged or pathetic was likelier to get me where I wanted.

"Where will I go?"

"You've got so many – friends to help you."

Yeah, maybe I could move in with Philip and Mrs Philip. Or Bernie, in his riverside mansion, in return for an endless supply of dirty pants. Actually that wasn't a bad plan. I stood up ponderously and went to my room, ignoring her whimpers and taking the oil heater. I needed to think.

Chapter Three

When men ask how I got into this business, they always want to hear some fantasy filth about the sexual awakenings of my teenage self, probably involving words like rosebud, pert, smooth, curious. Girls, though, are always keen to believe that I've been sexually abused. I'm terribly sorry, but not knowing my audience this time, I'm going to have to bore and disappoint almost all of you. Much of being a good stripper, dominatrix, sex worker of any description, really – is saying and being what your audience wants. I can't do that here. I suppose I'll just have to tell you the truth or something.

Anyway, I'm not writing this for you, but for me, so take the truth and stick it if it doesn't confirm your prejudices or give you a boner. I want to understand, for my sake, how I got here. Because here is where I seem to be. I'm 44 now, and I can hardly go on pretending this is temporary; an extended summer job until my real life begins. No, this is me, my lot, for better or worse, until death us do part. I'm a sex worker. A proud cane carrying member of the world's oldest trade.

And it started the way most jobs do – or at least did, back in the day – I answered an ad in a local paper. It said:

'Dancers wanted! You will earn up to £600 a night. No experience necessary.'

That was it. Well, I liked dancing, I loved money, and I'd no experience of anything at all, so it seemed perfect. Certainly more interesting than all the admin clerks and care assistants and road crossing patrol attendants which were my other options. I rang up and was told to attend an audition. They held auditions every night at 5 p.m., turnover being so high, and men's appetite for new girls so insatiable. I was to attend the Windmill, just off Piccadilly Circus. My mum was very impressed when I told her. She'd worked in variety herself, so the prospect of her only child jiggling for cash rather pleased her, not to mention the mention of the nightly £600.

Now, I wasn't a total idiot. I was reasonably confident that earning £600 a night would involve more than a few high kicks on a sparkly stage. But – well – I just thought, why not? I had just left Oxford University, having gone rather mad after a year of abuse. (State school girls don't make it to Oxford for a reason: they'd just hate it. It's a kindness, mark my words. Letting a girl from an Essex comp go to Oxbridge is like putting a pig into a Miss World contest – whether it's meant as a kindly gesture or a practical joke, it's not going to end well for the pig.) It seemed I had nothing to lose. I didn't know who I was any more, or what I wanted. My whole life plan had gone to cock. What should I have done? The bald facts remained. I liked dancing, I liked money, I had little of either in my life and – so why the hell not?

Ah, but it's a dangerous question, this 'Why the hell not?'. It could have led me to far darker places than the Windmill. I was lucky. I wasn't a total idiot, but I was still, in all fairness, a bit of an idiot. So much so I turned up for my audition in leggings, jazz shoes and a leotard. I quickly realised my mistake when I saw the other girls in heels, corsets and miniskirts. But I was buggered if I was going to back out now, having spent all day working myself into a nervous frenzy about what I was getting myself into. Anyway, the other girls were sweethearts. We bonded. There were three students (from Goldsmiths – it really does seem extraordinary and disproportionate how many strippers hail from Goldsmiths), an Aussie backpacker, and a woman in her thirties who hoped to revive her florist shop with a cash injection.

We all talked for hours, waiting for the owner, Oscar, to return. He'd been delayed at court, apparently. We never did learn why he was there in the first place. It all seemed quite glamorous to my 19-year-old self, rather than terrifying, as it might now. Honestly, I can't remember what we talked about, but I remember feeling happy, and accepted. No one judged you here. We were the dross, we had nowhere left to fall, nothing to prove. We were all money hungry, one and all, and prepared to sell viewing rights to some of the flaps and folds we'd been born with, to fund our studies, our businesses, our children, our travel. We discussed them all, our needs and plans, and decided what we'd do with the money (£600 a night! £3600 a week! In 1995!) just as soon as the owner came back from court and saw us, and hired us on the spot.

We waited an hour. Oscar's son gave us a bottle of wine. We waited and talked some more. The florist talked about how hard it was running a business and looking after her kids now her fella had left her. The students talked about trying to keep themselves fed and housed in London on a student loan. The Aussie backpacker, a gorgeous girl with ginger corkscrew curls, had done it all before, all of it, and talked about how she saw each man as a walking, grinning giant dollar sign. She was the only one with any experience. The rest of us were clueless.

At 8pm Oscar showed up, charming, dark, glamorous, full of apologies. We were all pretty drunk by then, having sneaked a few extra bottles from behind the impressively stocked, charmingly unattended bar. We were told to walk out onto the stage from the wings, remove our tops, and then walk off again. This would, presumably, allow Oscar to gauge our capacity for embarrassment, and our stage presence, along with our tits. I loved walking out on that stage. I felt powerful, delirious with excitement, knowing all eyes were on me. But I also knew I hadn't a hope of being accepted, after struggling for some minutes with my leotard to produce a pair of rather pendulous, disappointing knockers. I went through with it, and watched excitedly as my friends bounced out of their sequinned corsets. I knew I hadn't got the job, knew it even before Oscar kindly instructed his secretary to take all our names and numbers, whilst surreptitiously pointing to the three he wanted. (Two students, one backpacker. Not the florist. I wonder whatever happened to her? Bet she didn't save the business. If only I'd met her today, I would tell her to take up domination immediately.)

I knew he didn't want me. I knew I'd wait in vain for a call that wouldn't come. And I knew, having had a taste of this life – wine, sequins, stages, girls with a cracking line in conversation and nothing at all to lose – that I wanted it all for myself. I knew it like I've never known anything before or since. This was where I belonged. I was a whore to the bone. And I was right too. So many people waste years trying to figure out what they are and where they belong. I was super lucky to get it all sorted out before I turned 20. I invested in some pretty underwear, hold ups, Ann Summers knickers, a lacy black dress from C&A that I actually still possess – just ask, and I'll show it to you some day. I went back the next night, in heels and a push-up bra, and wiggled my tits, nipples perked up with lip gloss, right in Oscar's face. Somehow I oozed confidence. Something about being on stage, having eyes upon me, made that happen. I can't explain it. But it was true then and remains so. Somehow, I only felt I owned myself, my body, my space, when someone else was watching. It's not feminist, I admit it sounds a little creepy, but it still happens to be the bloody truth. So sit on it and swivel.

That time, I got the job.

Chapter Four

Opening Onlyfans, I found I'd a new subscription and been sent an image by a chap with classic paedo features – puffed out sweaty head, greasy hair, enormous glasses. And that was his profile picture. The image would be of his cock, presumably. One day I'll be sent a picture of someone's apple pie or Doberman and I'll pass out and bang some sense into my brains. I clicked. Cock filled the screen. I tilted it away from the do-gooder. A perfectly average cock, standing aloft over bulging, hairy gut. Um. Well, he's paying, so I'll play.

"Gosh, that's gorgeous! Wow!"

"Really?"

"Oh yes!"

"How big do you think it is?"

Ah. You'd think that would be a straightforward question. In fact it's as fraught as guessing a woman's weight.

"Oh – at least seven or eight inches, I'd say. A whopper!"

Typing.

"No. It's tiny."

Bollocks. Jumped the wrong way. Well, better that than the reverse.

"Only five inches." Average. Called it. Idiot. "Tiny balls too. And I'm a virgin. What would you like me to do to your cock mistress?"

"That tiny useless thing?" What, what? More pictures, a video, a wank? "You should slam it in a fridge door!"

"Why???"

Christ, I'm losing my knack. "Only kidding! A lovely long wank! Send me a video. Say my name as you come."

"Another drink?" Do-gooder peered into my space and I slammed the laptop shut.

"That would be wonderful. Thank you. I'll babysit again."

"It's medieval torture this time. You might find that more to your taste." He left me staring at his excellent arse, open-mouthed, before my gaze slid to the screen. Whipping, screaming. He wasn't wrong. He stood at the bar, demonstrating the kind of pleasant patience that gets you served faster, like they teach you in schools you pay for. Surrounded by brass and velvet and flashing lights, an incongruous beast in a gilded cage. The barmaid squirmed and responded to his charm with indecent speed, before I'd had time to read all I pleased.

I'd been spending more time here, leaving Katie turning her flat into a vulgar little fuck pad, still trying to think what to do, and oft as not the do-gooder was here, typing busily. We'd got into a thing of sharing work space and buying rounds. I drank rather quicker than him, so it was sort of saving cash and calories. And it was companionable, having a body beside me. Made me actually buckle down and do some work, rather than spend my spare time stalking rivals on Twitter. I had even got so far as to place an ad for a kinky landlord on Fetlife, and fend off a few thousand of the inevitable weirdos who'd responded. A crisis had been foisted on me: well, I would explore it, I would even exploit it. Who knew what this next chapter of my life might bring? Shouldn't be boring, anyway.

"Was I right?" A sparkly new pint caught my eye.

"Hmm? Oh. Thanks."

"What are you up to, anyway?"

I dislike being asked direct questions, and tend to lie when assaulted with them. "I'm writing to my mother."

"Is she well?"

"Extremely. Thank you."

"Smashing."

I watched his neat lips pronounce the word, expensive little teeth, firm chin, those frighteningly blue eyes, downy skin, like a girl – did he even need to shave? – then, letting my eyes roam below the face, enjoyed his posture and physique like the old perv I've become. I adjusted my thigh to press against his. All muscle, as I'd thought. The discovery I could still find a man interesting was rather refreshing. I clinked his glass with mine.

"And you?"

"Writing. I'm a freelance features writer."

"How quaint. Surely there's no money in that."

"I seek truth, not money." How his eyes danced at that witticism.

"That sounds like a lie. And surely a lie told with good intent can be more revealing than the truth? Certainly more interesting."

"Did you enjoy the medieval torture? It's for a Halloween piece."

"It was definitely a step up from the refugees."

"Are you a rabid right-winger?"

"Not in the least. I haven't the energy to be a rabid anything. But altruism is the most unforgivable of lies. It's barely concealed aggression."

"I think it's important to try to understand other cultures and people and their plight."

"Really? No you don't. That's how you'd like to be thought of, perhaps. No one really cares about strangers."

"More lies, eh?"

"All communication is essentially fiction. Actions may not lie. Words can't help but deceive. They mean such different things to different people."

"What are you really doing here?"

"I've told you."

"For two weeks? You must be a very close family."

"Christ, has it been that long?"

I opened my machine again rather pointedly and set to work tackling emails. There was a girl in Derby looking for a flatmate. Nice enough flat, and cheap too, but she seemed to be a working girl, and together we might reasonably be considered to be running a brothel, even though with my clients the sex happened only in their heads. This was probably too subtle a distinction to carry much weight with the police, of whom mercifully I'd so far managed to steer clear.

Perhaps I should get a proper job. But the prospect sounded worse than death, and anyway, how did one do it? I'd had the very occasional brush with respectability, but never kept it up long enough to please a landlord. Wouldn't I need to spend three months engaged in some menial labour before a rental agency would accept I was sufficiently human to warrant having a home, or something? And how would I even get a job after all this time, with no experience I could admit to? The real world frightened me. People expecting hours of your day from you, forcing you to do mysterious things, not even trying to hide their disappointment at your lack of ability. My only real skill was being charming to people I hated, although only for two hours maximum. I could probably do something suited to a refugee, actually – caring, or cleaning, perhaps. That might be soothing. I could talk well enough. Maybe sales.

A message from Katie popped up.

"Want to go rollerblading tonight?"

I snorted. Journo glanced up from his furious editing.

"Live with a person for two years, they still know nothing about you."

"Well, in fairness, you're hardly forthcoming."

I ignored this, since Katie was busily making another facile suggestion. "And have you considered contacting Robert? He's still in that big old house all on his own. Surely you could come to an arrangement?"

Robert was my ex. Couldn't cope with me "going on dates with other men," and though I kept promising to stop, I never did, and he would keep finding out, so we parted. But he was still lonely and heartbroken and all that and probably would house me, in return for some company at the weekend and me fussing over him a bit. He was of an age to need it. Cursed daddy issues. Couldn't work there though. Still, beggars and all that. I continued to ignore Katie, because she had ruined my life and deserved to be ignored. Robert would be troublesome, no doubt, but he'd be gagging to have me and it would mean I could settle this rather boring problem and move on.

"You have the most readable face, for someone who so values their privacy."

"Was I beaming?"

"You were beaming."

"I've decided to surrender my pride for the good of my career."

"Surely no decent career would demand that?"

"Well. Define decent."

"What is it you do?"

"I'm a sex worker."

He rolled his eyes and returned to his typing.

"Ah, but it's true. Nothing finer, actually. More honest than all that shit they teach you at school. Work hard, study, pass your exams, you'll get a good job and live a good life. Bollocks you will. Horse shit. For girls like me that isn't an option. Decent universities aren't geared up for working class kids, shy, diffident, anxious. Sex work is the only possible happy outcome for a working-class girl. God knows what boys are meant to do. Sell drugs I guess. Not my problem, thank God. For girls, you can either rely on one man and perpetually fear he'll abandon you, or rely on all men, and be confident you'll be to the taste of enough of them that you can make a living. And don't doubt it, you will be. Fat thin old young plain crippled scarred smelly. They will always love you in sufficient quantity you need never work again, not proper graft, no, nor worry about keeping one man happy and faithful, which is downright bastard impossible."

"I didn't say anything."

"Gee, I wonder why the world is so down on sex work, when women controlling and utilising their own sexuality can bring them such satisfaction and wealth? It's almost as if someone somewhere had a vested interest in keeping women down. But I'm not a feminist, you understand. The bitches wouldn't have me for one thing. Fraternising with the enemy, giving men what they want, I'm to be first up against the wall when the revolution comes."

"You've stopped beaming."

"I hate feeling judged by people who–" But there I stopped, for calling him privileged would be undignified and cowardly. "By anyone. Realising nothing you want or deserve is ever going to come your way – that's the only possible revolution, I say. Proper liberating too."

"Once you start telling the truth, you don't stop, do you?"

"I so regret all the years I spent in education. Years and years. Such a criminal waste. There was nothing waiting for me in a classroom but a new consciousness of my own misery, a recognition of the paucity of my own future. Simpleton that I was, then, I swallowed all their wicked lies whole. I was young and stupid and vulnerable enough to think teachers knew best – qualities that could have earned me a damn fortune before I turned twenty, if only I'd laid down my books and picked up a thong."

"You have given this speech before, I suspect."

"For people like me, education is a mocking cruelty. It will only ever teach you what you can't have. Oh sure, you could work hard and become a teacher yourself, I guess, perpetuate the cruelty, the myths, the time-wasting lies, feed them to children who will never, never, no matter what, amount to anything. But thrashing bloodied buttocks seems a lot less savage."

"So you're a dominatrix?"

"Disciplinarian. I'm no good at all that thigh high PVC boots and nipple tassels malarkey. Strict aunt, teacher, mum, wife, that sort of caper. Domestic discipline." It was a treat to talk about it, actually.

"So what have you decided to do for the good of your career?"

"Oh. That. Move back in with my ex. Getting accommodation is always an issue. Being kicked out of my current place, and, well, the world isn't really geared for the cash economy any longer."

"You could get a different job!"

"Pah!" I said, emphatically, even though I had literally just been thinking that, because I'd talked myself deep into a self-righteous frenzy. "Who'd have me?"

Chapter Five

I was selling vibrating hairbrushes at Waterloo station when I got the call from the Windmill. Selling hairbrushes was a simple job and I rather liked it, but now it was December it was decidedly cold standing on the concourse all day. Plus, I seemed to have an unfailing knack for attracting nutters. My colleagues were charming, though – Tara worked with me on hairbrushes while Sam demonstrated snoods – and I'd told them all about my audition. They were just as excited as me when my phone rang.

"Hello?" I fumbled desperately at my hairbrush, which made an astonishing noise, trying to find the off switch.

"Clara? This is Ellen, the Windmill's housemother…"

"Ah, yes?" I tried to sound nonchalant, and keep my phone out of sight of the boss, while waving frantically at passers-by with my hairbrush. Beside me, Tara saw my difficulty and tried to provide a distraction by shouting as loudly as possible "Luvverly hairbrushes! Cure baldness! Give massages! Make hair shine! Good for Christmas!"

"We'd like you to come in tonight for a trial run, and if you get along alright, look to taking you on permanently…"

Yesss! I did a little victory dance for Tara's benefit, which a passing lunatic promptly began to ape.

"Pop by at 8 or so and Sven will show you the ropes. Bring plenty of makeup and a couple of outfits – oh, and a garter belt…"

Resolutely I turned my back on the gathering crowd, trying to take in what I was being told. What was a garter belt again?

"Your shift finishes at 3.30 a.m., and we expect to see you here six nights a week. You'll pay £25 a night to work here."

Eh? That was what I earned selling hairbrushes all day! And I'd have to be back at Waterloo at 7 a.m. to keep doing it. I could probably make it, as long as I didn't feel the need to sleep, ever.

"So, see you tonight. And Clara – what is your stage name? I'll need to write it down for the DJ…"

Stage name? Christ, of all the things I hadn't ever dreamt I'd have to worry about. I gazed thoughtfully at Tara, beaming encouragement at me even as she buzzed her brush enthusiastically over a bald scalp, and came to a snap decision.

"Clara – that's my stage name."

Pause. "Oh, right. I see. So what's your real name then, or would you rather not say?"

Oh god, what? Emerald, Crystal, Sprinkles, Gypsy?

"Exactly, yes. I prefer to stay Clara – more … professional, you know?"

"Right you are. See you tonight then. 'Clara'."

I was pretty sure her inverted commas were ironic, but I didn't care. I'd got the bloody gig! Money, sequins, somewhere warm and alcoholic to spend my evenings! I did another little dance, and promptly sold more hairbrushes, purely on the back of my extraordinary enthusiasm.

Sam, on snoods, regarded me with the world-weary cynicism of a mature 22-year-old. "You get sex job?" I nodded excitedly. He was Russian. That's a Russian accent I'm doing there. So was Tara. Although when asked they both claimed to be Spanish.

"You never get away from sex job, once you start. You be sure you want this. I used to work door in brothel…" This was news! "… so I know. Good money, yes, but frightening too. Police, drugs, dogs, guns. Valium for breakfast. Pretty girls broken up. You be careful now."

He turned away ponderously. Well, brothels sounded a long way from elegantly lit dancing clubs to my young ears. They were legal, for a start, and tightly regulated, swarming with bouncers. But I've often thought about Sam over the years, and how right he was. You never get away from sex job.

On her lunch break, Tara kindly fashioned me a makeshift garter belt from her laddered stocking. I slipped it into my bag, imagining it hung low with money. The money had started to take on life and shape in my imagination. I'd passed my driving test, but couldn't possibly afford a car. Pretty things, theatre tickets, treats for my mum, just the sheer raw pleasure of seeing your bank balance without gasping in horror, all started to seem possible. The prospect of passing a shop window without automatically averting one's eyes.

I sold thirteen hairbrushes that day, I remember, earning 65 p profit on each. I gave token help with packing away the stall for the evening, but Tara shooed me off to the loo to get myself ready. I only had one dress, my audition dress. I'd stuffed it hopefully into my rucksack that morning, along with my heels, and the few bits of makeup I possessed. I popped into Boots for a sandwich and a shiny dark red lip gloss, the colour of old blood. I applied it in the station toilet, making faces at myself, giddy with excitement. It didn't seem real, none of it. I put on my dress. It was ridiculously short for street wear. If I leant forward even an inch I'd be showing my breakfast, but I had no idea if I'd be able to change when I got there, or if I'd be straight out on stage. I looked ridiculously young and skinny in my new garb, like a China doll, or a teenage runaway. Sam whistled when he saw me. "You look…" he hesitated, rolled the word round his mouth, lips twitching, then decided to say it – "Sexy."

I'd never been called that before! My innocence, as it happened, was my chief asset, my USP. Shame it couldn't last.

I attracted quite a number of lustful glances as I trotted over to Piccadilly, and lapped them up. This, I thought, was the beginning of a new life – womanhood, riches, admiration, adventure! I sashayed into the club, pausing at the door to see if anyone was watching me. They weren't. Commuters bombed past, grey faced and hunched against the wind; a boy slipped into the phone box outside to post up the prostitutes' business cards. Well, well, I'd be noticed soon enough! I slipped inside, and hung about the empty reception for a bit, wondering what to do.

"New girl?"

A plump, blonde woman called to me from the bottom of a well-obscured flight of stairs.

"Yes, um… yes."

"The dressing rooms are down here, I'll show you."

She turned and began walking slowly, majestically, down the darkened corridor, a chubby Orpheus in slippers. Deep breath, chest out, I decided to follow her.

There were four dressing rooms in the club's bowels, and I was assigned to the third. This early in the evening they were devoid of girls ('100+, of all nationalities!!' the poster screamed), but they'd stamped their presence on the place – sequins and taffeta on the rails, feather boas on the coat hooks, the whiff of stale smoke, hairspray and perfume. It was airless, lined with mirrors and shelves, and the strip lighting was utterly unforgiving. I caught sight of myself and looked away hurriedly.

"Leave your stuff here, love. I'm Jackie, the house mum. That's my room over there." She pointed to a little cubby-hole, stacked with boxes of make-up, sweets and glitter.

"If you want to use my stuff, you pay a pound."

"I… brought some stuff to use…"

"Righto. You might find you need more than usual, though. The stage lights wash you out a bit." She peered at my face critically. I backed away and she laughed.

"Oh, you'll get used to that! You better go and see Steve now. He'll need to check your hair."

I trotted away obediently, wondering if Steve was the club's onsite hairdresser, and whether I'd be able to save money on my usual dry trims if so. Maybe he'd do something exciting with my limp brown locks – curl them, pin them up with diamante grips?

The club looked much more impressive by night, all glittery, full of dark, seedy looking corners. The stage itself was spectacular, with a huge shiny pole whose purpose I couldn't even start to fathom, a hundred or so tables laid out around it, and at the back, a huge standing area around the bar from which the stage was barely visible. Later I learned that using these tables incurred a fantastic cover fee, which explained why they were generally empty till after midnight, when people were too drunk to care. A DJ's box stood beside the stage, where a man with a greying mullet was writing furiously. He saw me and waved.

"Hulloo!"

"Hello! Um. Do you know where Steve is?" I shouted.

"Probably in his office" the man yelled back, unhelpfully. "Are you Clara?"

"Yes!"

"Well you can't be Clara, we've already got a Clara. Do you have another name?"

"Er …" My mind went blank. Again. You might think I'd have spent the intervening hours thinking up more suitably glamorous names, but apparently not. My middle name was Rosie, but I never admitted it to anybody.

"Most of the girls," he continued bellowing cheerfully, "use the name of their ex's new girlfriend!"

Oh. Well, I didn't have an ex, just an on-off, love-struck idiot who would doubtless inconveniently kill himself if I ever left him, rather than shacking up with fresh lap-dancer name material.

I stared helplessly. The DJ tutted. Then screeched:

"Tell you what, do you have a tattoo?"

"No!"

"Alright then, you can be 'Clara without the tattoo'. When you hear that you need to get on stage. Got it?"

I got it. And 'Clara *with* the tattoo', a short, sweet New Zealander with a giant scorpion on her left buttock, was kind enough to share her name. Sometimes, even now, I introduce myself as Clara Without the Tattoo at PTFA meetings. I found Steve in the end, a dark, sallow man in a bow tie, a debonair Dracula who never smiled or slept.

"Clara? Welcome. Can you drop your knickers and lift your skirt?"

Ah well, here we go, I thought: this way to the white slave trade. I'd have to shag him to get the job, then I'd be trafficked into some Far Eastern brothel when my cunt grew too loose for the Western market: every job has its downside. I did as he asked. He frowned at my groin.

"You're a bit bushy. You need to trim up the sides a bit more."

He ran an experimental finger over my curls, and I gave a little shiver of fear, or excitement, or something. This is how it would be from now, I thought: constantly being judged and found wanting. But only physically, which made a nice change from A-levels.

"Underwear's fine. Turn round, bend over."

For a minute, I wondered if he was going to finger my arse, like a prospective owner, and whether I'd let him, or if that would be my cue to walk out. But he didn't. I felt the surge of righteous anger drain from me.

"Your bottom's a bit hairy too. You need to sort that out as soon as possible. But you'll do for tonight."

I pulled up my pants and turned to face him, still staring at me insolently.

"Novelty value, perhaps."

Sensing my interview was at an end, I drifted away and stood in a corner, feeling myself an awkward mass of limbs, without any idea of what to do with them. The other girls were starting to arrive now, bustling about, loud and important. They were a curious looking bunch, with no prevalent physical type. Fat and thin, young and old, blonde and brunette; I wondered how anyone ever got rejected. I suspect now it was confidence, charisma, stage presence that Oscar was after, rather than mere good looks.

A girl in her late 30s with long red hair and enormous tits was sitting at a table, and smiled up in my direction as she spotted me trying to blend in against the wall.

"Alright love? New are yer? Don't worry, you'll soon get used to it all. I'm Shona."

"Clara."

"Pleased to meet yer."

Her accent was broad Liverpudlian. As I watched, she began painting her nails with a metallic purple polish, whilst surreptitiously sneaking bites at a cream cheese bagel whenever the bar staff weren't watching.

"So…" I swallowed, "How long have you been here?"

"Four months. It's alright. Hard work, but you do earn. I'm buying my own house."

"Oooh!" I said, since it seemed to be required.

She nodded. "I'm doing a grand a week at least, so it shouldn't take long. Then I can go back home. How about you?"

"Oh, I'm – a student. On a gap year." Which was true enough; I'd told my 'moral tutor' at Oxford I'd be back in September, having taken a year away to become less insane and teary, a prospect he welcomed.

"So – what do I do?"

She shrugged. "Just wander around and talk to them. You get £35 an hour for talking, £10 for a table dance – that's just down to underwear, you need to stay three feet away from them, they're dead strict – or £20 on stage for full nudity." Except she pronounced it "Nudd-ity."

"We used to get commission on champagne, but they've just stopped that. Shit, innit?" as she saw my face fall. "But you're still expected to rack up a massive bar bill. Ask for champagne. If they won't stretch to that, go for wine. You'll still get plenty of drink, don't worry. They won't keep you if you don't."

"And you still have to pay the £25?"

"Oh yeah. Don't worry about that, you'll make it easy. Just think of it as tax." She chortled at the thought. But I was worried. I didn't have £25 on me, or in the world, and the thought that I might end this peculiar night in debt as well as humiliated was simply horrifying.

"And what's it like, dancing on stage?"

She shrugged. "S'alright. You get used to it quick enough. Don't even think about it after the first time. But you can watch me first, if you want. My regular's here."

A bashful young man had just slipped in the door, and instantly Shona's posture changed: in one smooth move she brushed away the crumbs, concealed her polish, stuck out her tits, and offered her most dazzling smile. I watched, entranced, as he bought her wine, and moved with her, arm in arm, down to the stage, where she slunk up the stairs and began to move. Not dance: there was no dance involved with Shona. She squatted down on her knees and moved back and forth. She licked her fingers and tweaked her nipples, then seemed to slip her finger into her admirably neat front garden. She moaned and rocked in time to the music – roughly – while her young man watched, entranced. It was much ruder, and much stranger, than I could possibly have envisaged. Thank God she didn't go anywhere near that bloody pole. But I couldn't help but worry about the hygiene issues of stroking your fingers on that dusty stage, then sticking them inside yourself – never mind shaking hands with the fella afterwards, as Shona was now doing.

She grinned at me as she walked past, dragging her punter back to the bar, as if to say "See? Piece of piss." Certainly it didn't look difficult. I had no doubt I could do something similar, should the opportunity present itself. I just hoped to God it would.

The place was starting to full up now, and I watched the other girls, dozens of them, glittery, stiff-haired, prowling and pouncing on the men with great shiny lipstick smiles. I gulped, checked my lipstick, and decided to make a start myself.

"Hello, I'm Clara," I announced, rather too loudly, to a fat, balding chap I thought looked unthreatening, like a favourite uncle.

"Eh? Sorry love. I'm only here for Jasmine. New, are you? You'll be seeing a lot of me."

He gave a throaty laugh and slapped me affectionately on the shoulder. Definitely the affectionate uncle type, then, but sadly, not my uncle. I watched Jasmine sidle up to him, to be greeted by noisy kisses, a roll of notes, and a bottle of champagne.

Arse. Well, maybe I'd have my own regular soon! I tried again. But while I met some charming men, I also got to hear some standard rejections. They'd just arrived. They were just having a look round. They wouldn't be staying long. Nice men, in silk ties and gold cufflinks, who spoke beautifully, through neat white teeth that had been nurtured by the finest dentists, and rejected me over and over again, with honeyed words and elegant smiles. I didn't know what to do. My feet ached in their unaccustomed heels, and my face hurt from smiling. I didn't have the right words, not yet. I wandered around the club, learning its geography, the pool rooms, the balconies, the quiet private booths. I drifted down to the dressing rooms to re-do my make-up. I gave myself a little pep talk in the mirror.

The house mother was very sympathetic.

"It's just a numbers game, my lovely. The more you talk to, the likelier you are to get a hit."

I'd heard something similar from my vibrating hairbrush supervisor. I nodded earnestly, and redoubled my resolve. Plates of cheese sandwiches had appeared to help the girls mop up their champagne intake. I took three, determined to get me some champagne to justify them.

Bloated but invigorated, I click-clicked back up the stairs, just in time to hear the DJ calling "Clara without the tattoo, on stage in two minutes please." Oh glory! And the club was teeming with bodies now, too: in my absence another hundred or so fellas had arrived, brand new quarry, moneyed, drunk – and expecting a show. I pulled on the arm of the nearest.

"That's me – I'm 'Clara without the tattoo'!"

"Oh yes?" he said, politely, a young chap, pink cheeks, eyes gleaming with excitement and beer.

"Well – er – good luck. I look forward to seeing what you can do."

"No, but, I mean, I've never done it before, it's my first time. I've never been… naked… in public."

"Really?" Clearly he thought this was a line.

"Really!" Luckily the DJ cut in to confirm it.

"'Clara without the tattoo' to the stage now please, for her debut performance here at the Windmill, or, indeed anywhere in the world… 'Clara without the tattoo'."

"Blimey! Well, gosh!" Bless him, he handed me his whiskey, which I gulped back with an attempted air of nonchalance, although in truth I nearly brought it straight back up.

"And how are you feeling?"

"Terrified," I said, immediately, and after a moment's thought, "Excited too, I think." More to myself than to him I added, "I wish to God I hadn't had those sandwiches."

But then the DJ saw me and started waving his arms in a manner I could only interpret as angry, so I had to leave this sweet boy man who suddenly seemed my best friend in the whole world, and take the long walk to the stage.

Now, I can dance. The dancing part, I thought, would be easy. It was just the logistics that worried me: how long before I started to disrobe, how much should I show, what if I couldn't manage to undo my bra? Should I show each bit of me to each bit of the audience, like a magician will his deck of cards? How would I manage to retrieve all my clothes and leave the stage starkers whilst retaining an air of elegance and mystery, and reappear two minutes later to continue chatting to this boy man, whom I was now convinced would be my first hit?

But my music had started. I had chosen Madonna's 'La Isla Bonita', since I knew it quite well and was reasonably confident it was short and snappy. I jogged on to the stage, heart pounding, and there gave my very best impression of a stripper. Like anyone else at their first day at work, I copied my colleagues as far as I could, faked confidence, and smiled broadly. And I absolutely loved it. I loved feeling the eyes on me, having the stage to myself, hearing the applause at the close. I seem to recall I gave a mock curtsey, found my clothes, and sashayed off stage, heart still hammering, more with excitement than fear, I was certain. And I wanted to do it again. I dressed as quickly as possible, and rushed back to boy man, but to my disgust he'd been completely colonised by another girl. But he did grin and give me a thumbs up.

Well, this was simply marvellous. I'd been here three hours, shown my tits to 200 strangers, and I'd be paying £25 for the privilege. Fanbloodytastic. I felt new found confidence stiffening my spine. I walked back over to a table I'd already approached three times, where two men were talking earnestly. Perhaps, I thought, they'd like a little light relief from their philosophising. I decided to try a direct approach.

"Hello? Hello! Hello? Would you two like a table dance?"

They broke off to stare at me. One gestured that I should leave. The other one reached into his pocket, found a note and thrust it at me, then gestured that I should leave. I did as I was bid, then, by the light of the bar, unfolded the bill. It was a $100 bill.

A $100 bill! I had only the vaguest ideas what that would mean, in fiscal terms. But it was the first money I had earned for being naked, and precious for that reason alone. I was reasonably confident it would cover my £25 fee, anyhow, and maybe even bring me a little profit! Never mind that I had been paid to go away: it was money, and I was glad of it, and it brought me confidence to try for more. I was given a £10 table dance, then another, then another, and a couple of £20 stage dances too. I had an hour's conversation with a hotelier, who gave me £40 for my time. I walked out of there with £85 English money, and my $100 bill: I had 'done a one-er' as the cabbies say, and I'd had a bloody ball. I'd also drunk more than I was accustomed to. At 3.30 a.m. I was released from my stint, and staggered back to Waterloo station, where I'd be needed for work the next day. I didn't need sleep, or transport, or protection: I felt utterly invincible. And at least I'd know to wear my jeans next time.

At 6 a.m. I was woken just outside the loos by a tramp, who told me politely that my purse was sitting right on top of my open bag, and that anyone might steal it. I sat up from the metal bench where I had snatched an hour's sleep, smoothed my hair, and handed him a pound for his trouble. Then I checked my purse. All that lovely money was still there. It seemed extraordinary that you could have a night out, dance and drink and gossip, and come back with £100 more than you had before. It still does, really.

The shops were starting to open at Waterloo. I went to Boots for deodorant and toothpaste, and the currency exchange place with my $100. They gave me £64.38. Unbelievable! Free money! What a laugh, what a swizz, what larks!

Chapter Six

Having made up my mind to go back to Robert there seemed no reason to delay. He was still in the house we bought together, living more or less the same life, only dustier and sadder, I assumed. I felt my guts clench as I drove down the suburban, net-twitchy, bungalow-heavy roads that lead to it. I'd set out like a knight on a noble quest, facing the past for the good of my future, but staring at my old front door (newly painted, the bastard) I felt more like a kicked dog, with no spirit, brains or imagination. I'd left him flamboyantly, triumphantly, planning great things, and I was back two years later having accomplished nothing new, nothing of note. Mind you, from my occasional stalking, nor had he.

Robert was a musician. He gave the odd lesson and played in a band – original, authentic, post-punk guff, which means he couldn't play weddings or pubs or do anything else that might actually make money, and was really in no position to complain about how I kept us. He valued authenticity before profit, which I found charming initially. I have a bad record when it comes to musicians. I find them oddly irresistible. Also artists, poets and actors. It's a shocking, self-destructive habit. Luckily this one also had rich doting parents, so he could carry on being authentic without worrying about the gas bill. My partners divide into two categories: either they are working class but terribly sensitive, well-read and arty; or middle class but abject fucking failures, into which category Robert obviously fell. Twenty-five years my senior, not in the best of health, but with dark curly hair he kept rather long, which gave an illusion of youth until you got close, like a shiny apple crawling with maggots.

I mean, not very like that, but a bit.

I still had a key. The door scraped noisily along the floor, then stuck, although not before my nose could be assailed by dust and the smell of old food. So he was still going in for that gone to seed, pathetic vibe. Good to know. Jesus now hung in the hallway. Mysteriously, I married a Christian. I find Christianity quite a compelling narrative – all that transformation through suffering stuff sets my inner masochist a quiver – but the mystical aspects are patently nonsense.

I found him buried in his music room. He stood up on seeing me, said, "Oh, shit," then beckoned to indicate I should sit in his chair, the only recognisable piece of furniture in the room, while he stood. I ignored him, so we both stood with the chair between us. He looked rather grey.

"The thing is, Robert" I said, as if the intervening two years hadn't happened, "I'm in a jam. Getting kicked out of my current place. So I wondered if you still had a spare room here, and how you'd feel about me moving in, if only for a short spell?"

I watched his brain whirr, his Adam's apple bob nervously about his throat.

"I won't work here, of course. It would literally just be a place to sleep."

"So – where…"

"I'll only do out calls," I said, hastily, thinking I was probably lying, and there would be a few French farce moments before I got chucked out again, but let tomorrow take care of itself. You'll have noticed already I don't really approve of truth, the slippery wee bastard. He was still staring at me like a concussed guppy and I was starting to suspect this was an idiotic idea. The caravan in Leysdown beckoned with glimmering allure.

"How are you, Robert? You look, well, much the same. Is there any wine?"

He cleared his throat. "No. I could go and get some though."

"You do that. Do you want some money?" I reached for my purse, but he jumped away from it as if it were possessed by a demon.

"I'll clear up the kitchen a bit, shall I?" A brisk, motherly tone might work best: authoritative, yes, but also caring.

"I'm sorry. If I'd known you were coming–"

"No, I'm sorry. Creature of impulse still, you know. Not to worry. We'll soon have this place shiny."

As soon as I get a slave in, that is.

I felt better with wine in my hand. The house was freezing as well as filthy. We clinked mugs. I stared at him.

"Well?"

"Surely I should be saying well?"

"Can I come back?"

"You know I want you to come back. I never wanted you to – go away."

"Yes, but this would be as housemates, you know. No emotional stuff. You do your work, I'll do mine. I do still own half this house."

"I know!" He rested his head in his hands.

"Well, are you going to be boring and troublesome about it?"

He straightened his chest. "No. No, of course you must come and live here. I would like it very much. Only – I don't want to hear anything about–"

"No. No, of course."

When he got back from his stag-do, Robert was pretty drunk. I hadn't seen him drunk before, not really. He's a cautious, careful man. He climbed into bed beside me and explained, cautiously, carefully, that if I ever left him for someone else, he would kill me. He told me at some length how he would rather spend the rest of his life in prison than spend it imagining me with someone else. I realised I was meant to find that frightening, and chastening. In fact, I found it rather arousing. I live to be wanted, usually. But this pathetic specimen was simply disgusting. Probably he'd been googling me again. I'd made some pretty mucky videos these last few weeks. High profile too, big studio stuff, often the very top of Pornhub's search results. I realised I shouldn't be proud of that, yet here we are.

We stood watching the rain smash horizontally against the panes, while both sneaking the occasional glance at the other. In the yellowy gloom, dressed in navy fisherman's jumper and tight black jeans, all rings and beads, he looked as though he were auditioning for a bit part in a rock musical: the shabby comical one, the hero's sidekick. He kept drumming his fingers against the table and mug, to some rhythm only he could follow, a habit that had incensed me throughout our marriage, and now made me ache.

He knew about the domination and porn and all that from the beginning. I don't hide any of it. Like I said, I'm pretty proud of what I do. If I'm interested in a chap I tell him quicker than most, since the knowledge they're sitting opposite a porn star generally thrills them. Not Robert. He blinked, pushed his glasses up his nose and continued to talk about music. I think I like the intensity of musicians. Also I like the way I make enough money to support us both, which gives me a (usually misguided) sense of security that the relationship might actually last. If they can't put diesel in their vans or purchase post-gig chips without me, that's some strong motivation to hang about. Not that it's ever worked that way, but ever the optimist, I feel surely one day it must.

Robert got on his knees, literally, and begged me to stop with the whoring. "I can't bear you going on dates with other men," he'd say, and I'd say, for heaven's sake, they're not dates, I'm thrashing them and pissing on them and taking their cash and throwing them out when the clock strikes the hour and if that's what happens on your dates you're possibly seeing the wrong women. But he wouldn't stop nagging me. Four years of it. Wears you down, I can tell you.

He'd covered our kitchen cupboards in pictures of his friends and family, a smorgasbord of smiles from which I was noticeably absent. History rewritten. He saw me looking, and turned his gaze towards me with the kind of tender exasperated concern with which women regard babies. He wanted to try again. He wanted to turn me into someone he could value. This was definitely a mistake. I put down the mug.

"Maybe we should just sell up, eh?"

"No! No. This is your home, our home. You must live here. I'll – it will be nice to have someone to look after."

"I won't need looking after, thank you. This is simply a practical arrangement."

"I love you." He said it as if it were a threat, clutching his drunk tight enough to whiten the knuckles. "I've suffered horribly these last two years."

"I'm sorry to hear that," I said, without troubling to sound convincing. "But you must understand how – how disgusting this sort of scene is. Your suffering is no concern of mine. Not any longer."

"We are still married."

"Not in any conventional sense."

"But in God's eyes."

"Oh, for fuck's sake." I slammed down my wine and wondered about storming off, although I couldn't quite find the energy, not yet. Beyond this now quite snug kitchen, where in time you got used to the worst of the smell, there was nothing waiting for me but a shit barn of a pub and a freezing flat where I wasn't wanted. Robert got on his knees before me, again, and looked up at me with big solemn eyes, like a calf about to be slaughtered.

"I shall change."

"There's really no need." I patted his head, and began to think what an amusing anecdote this would make for my blog. "I'll be back in the morning with my stuff. I can keep the canes in the car, if you'd rather. Yes. I'll do that," as he began to twist his hands rather violently. "Well if you wanted to give the place a little spruce tonight, if you're not too busy, that would be smashing. And now I must go and start packing." He held out his arms to me, toddler-like, and I gave him a stiff, unconvincing hug. "Alright, darling. Alright. Right you are, then. That's it. I'm going now. Back tomorrow, 10 a.m or so? Alright. Thanks for the drink. Bye darling. Bye." I extricated myself and snaked to the door, giving Jesus one long last unblinking stare.

Chapter Seven

I stayed at the Windmill for four months, and during that time some of my greenness began to subside. I met rock stars, politicians, media moguls, and Michael Schumacher, whom I infuriated by asking what he did for a living ("I'm a very famous racing driver!"). I danced for soldiers and city boys, journalists and vintners. I was offered jobs, cars, jewellery, tit jobs and cash for sex, all of which I politely declined. I got a handful of regulars myself – a financial adviser, a chap who worked on the *Daily Mail*, a property entrepreneur. I didn't like any of them particularly, but they seemed oddly keen on me. Most of the punters infuriated me, honestly. I'm no good at sitting and talking for hours on end, but often that was the only way I could make money. Once they've seen your flaps and folds they tend not to be over-bothered about seeing them again. Instead I had to listen to them spew vitriol about their wives and bosses. But I didn't mind that so much: more sickening, I found, was when they took an interest in me. I felt sullied by their enthusiasm for my youth, innocence, inexperience. So many of them wanted to cure me, to interpret my career choice as some sort of symptom, an erotically charged cry for help. Like Roger, the NLP expert.

It had been a dreadful night: all 70 girls out in force, perhaps 12 men between us, and only two hours before the rent was due. I had given up, and was doing a crossword with Alison, a girl I'd warmed to for being slightly younger and even less popular than me. She was skinny and angular with long black curls, like an ill-thought-out boy, and she had a charming habit of offering fully nude dances for 'bus fare' even though bartering and undercutting the other girls was strictly forbidden. That night, she hadn't earned a bean, so I, from the relative comfort of my £40 from my *Daily Mail* fella, was thrilled to see a tall beardy man beckoning her over, pointing to a waiting glass of champagne.

"You're in there, my lovely," I said, cheerfully putting my feet up into the space she had vacated and getting back to my crossword. She sprang across the room, all curls and eagerness, and returned a minute later full of dejection, to shove the champagne under my nose.

"He – he just wanted me to bring you this. B…because you look so sad."

"Oh, for fuck's sake. What a raging scrotal sack of septicaemia," I said, while smiling politely and mouthing 'Thank you' in his direction. He smiled back and toasted me.

"What does he think this is, an overstocked waitress convention? Don't you worry, gorgeous, I'll go over there and screw some money out of that ill-mannered cuntwipe, and bring it back to you, OK?"

My language had deteriorated with impressive rapidity. Alison smiled.

"You don't have to do that…"

"Course I do." And I marched off to meet the fuckety fucking fucktard.

"Thank you so much," I beamed, extending a hand and moving in for a peck on the cheek, the only permitted physical contact. "My name's Clara. And you are?"

"Roger. I just couldn't bear to see how sad you looked. I thought I'd try to make you a little happier."

He spoke in squeaky, well-bred tones that had clearly cost thousands of pounds and centuries of in-breeding.

"Well, that's very sweet of you! But I'm not sad, Roger, just a little bored, perhaps. There are so few men here and it's been ages, literally minutes, since I've had a chance to get my tits out, and they're starting to feel over-warm…"

He shook his head at me. "Oh, there's no need for that with me! You just don't want to be here, do you? Tell me, where would you rather be?"

Well obviously I don't want to be *here*, you cretin, talking to you, I'd quite like to be in my bed, or sitting next to Alison working on 12 down, or even, at a push, talking to my *Daily Mail* man, who had an amusing line in tittle-tattle and a vicious tongue. But truth wouldn't get Alison her bus fare. Roger grabbed my chin rather painfully.

"I can make your dreams come true!"

Oh Lord. Spare me the mean, spare me the bored, but above all, spare me the lunatics. I'd landed myself with the holy trinity.

"Um…"

"Nothing's too big if you know how to dream big!"

"I'd like to be…"

"Yes?"

"Richer?"

"Of course!" He gave my chin a congratulatory tweak. "Of course you would. Who wouldn't? All you have to do is imagine it!"

"Oh. Really?"

"Imagine a nice big fat sum of money. Imagine opening your bank statement and seeing, ooh, tens of thousands of pounds written in black at the bottom! Imagine it! Now!"

"But surely a more practical step would involve your buying a table dance…"

"Now!"

A small crowd was beginning to gather at his squealing, and I could feel Oscar's eyes on me. Oscar did not approve of scenes. I thought I'd better do as I was told. I shut my eyes for thirty seconds or so, smiled at the finish, then looked up to see him smiling encouragingly at me.

"See? Didn't that feel great?"

"Mmm. Ooh, I feel, oh, ever so inspired to go and earn a few a few more tenners right now…"

"You're thinking too small!" he shrieked, digging his fingernails back into my chin. "Do it ten more times!"

Oh Christ.

"Ten? Seriously? Wow, that's a lot. Ten? Right now?"

"If you're serious about accumulating wealth, yes."

He nodded, folded his arms and waited for me to begin. And Oscar crept closer, his piercing blue eyes on my face, lizard-like, unblinking, warning me to do as I was told. So I stood there, for ten minutes, faking concentrating hard, and adding a sudden flourish of excitement at the end. Ten times. A huge crowd of pissed up city boys turned up halfway through, so I could have been actually *making* money if I hadn't been stuck making a tit of myself next to this weirdo. Still, maybe the power of my positive thought had dragged them in.

"Well, that was thrilling, thank you so much. There is a hostess fee of…"

"Oh, you needn't pay me anything! The pleasure was all mine. Good luck Clara!"

And Roger bounded off into the night. Alison made her bus fare, and I made a few extra quid myself. We walked down to the night bus stop together, and while standing, shivering in the queue, both got covered in vomit emanating from the drunk behind us. Explain that, Roger, I thought; for I certainly didn't dream it.

The rot started to set in at the end of January. The first few weeks after Christmas we had a steady trickle of men, delighted to be free from the stifling, constant presence of their wives and families. But by the end of the month the credit card bills had started coming in, I guess. Certainly mine had. Suddenly the chief difficulty of the night wasn't staying sober enough to find your bus stop, nor trying to remember the name of the man with whom you'd spent several hours in intimate conversation the night before. No, the problem was simply trying to get through several dreary hours of nothingness. The girls started to bicker, out of boredom. We weren't allowed books, reasonably enough. Nor were we allowed to sleep in the dressing rooms. We had to stay in the club, watching and waiting, in case a man appeared: although the sight of 70 girls staring up at him hungrily would surely send most men screaming for the hills. Oscar let us all off paying our fees most nights, in the knowledge that most of hadn't made it. Lots of girls left. Lots more were fined for petty infractions of the rules. (Playing pool topless was banned, for heaven's sake! Although it was a fun way to earn a few quid, and actually I was getting quite good at pool.) With my posh voice and girl next door looks I was considered too risible to be worthy of firing. I clung on at the edges, waiting for it to get better. I missed the money. How quickly it started to feel normal flouncing home with a wallet crammed with tenners!

I'd been meeting a few idiots too. I'd probably been taking a slightly feistier approach, out of desperation, and I'd met a few unpleasant, bolshy types in consequence. I spent five hours talking to one chap, who refused to give me anything when I refused to go home with him afterwards (and he was the most ghastly, dull, arrogant wanker I've ever encountered in 25 years of punters). One drunken buffoon spat on me when I suggested a table dance. His spit dripped down my dress, purple satin, formerly a favourite. I spat back, hitting his tie, and he giggled like an imbecile.

But it was Valentine's night that finished me. It was a Saturday, and they were always dreadful anyway: we thrived on the after-work crowd showing off and cutting deals, all of whom sped off to Cornwall cottages of a Friday night. I'd assumed Valentine's would be particularly bad, but no one came in at all until midnight. Finally, half a dozen city boys showed up, drunk and braying, staggering into furniture while the girls circled them like piranhas. I hung back, confident I wouldn't be their type, and anyway I had my period and hated taking my knickers off, paranoid that the laser beam lights would show up the bits of blue sponge I'd shoved up my leaky gash. Anyway, one of the girls was teaching me to knit.

One of them came bumbling over to me, fat, sweaty, a line of dribble drying on the corner of his blubbery lips.

"Oi oi oi!"

"Oh, hello, how do you do?" I said frostily. My accent became ever more clipped in proportion to the vileness of its recipient.

"That – bloke…" he said, trying and failing to steady himself on my shoulder, while gesturing at the barman, "… said you had a hairy fanny."

"Oh yes?" I had no idea the bar staff ever looked at my genitals. They hid it well, but the place was dark, in fairness. And – I think I had done a drunken table dance on top of the actual bar the week before, unless that had been a dream. The barman threw me a sheepish grin whilst slamming a vodka and schnapps into a shaker.

"Have you… have you… got a hairy fanny? Minge? Cunt? Hairy cunt? Have you got a hairy cunt?"

He staggered into my face as he said it. I could smell him, sweat and money, and revulsion rose in me like nausea.

"Get off me" I said, and pushed him rather firmly in the shoulder. He fell backwards and hit his head on a table. I think he may have lost consciousness for a second or two. Then he lay there, giggling. A bouncer turned up and lugged him out of the club, while his mates bellowed abuse at me. I was a psychopath, a bitch, a cunt, a cock-tease. I'd had enough, I decided. If I wanted to suffer that kind of abuse I could have stayed at bloody Oxford. There was some kind of row going on in the dressing room, so it was easy enough to slip on my jeans and coat, pick up my bag, and quietly walk out, keeping my £25 for myself. So out I went, and treated myself to dinner and a taxi.

Chapter Eight

They've pretty much given up talking about hell in church. It's all cosy placatory drivel now, clapping, hugs, guitars. Shame. The idea of hell seemed a great consolation once, along with the wrathful God who'd send you there for eternity. A God who'd first tricked you into committing some obscure risible sin, then allowing his son to be tortured to death in a bid to save you from same obscure risible sin: when that didn't totally work, because why would it, allowing the quality saved people to watch the eternal torment of sinners from the comfort of heaven, for their own personal pleasure. And here's a fun twist: anyone who doesn't believe this wretched nonsense gets banged up for a fiery eternity too, along with the gays. Show me the domme who could think up any scenario as bloody perverse as that.

Robert and I are in church, a two hour marathon, featuring much whooping. The coffee is excellent and they give out free muffins and watermelon slices, I shit you not, but then tithing is basically obligatory. Thank God Robert has sod all to share. The tunes are catchy. Sometimes he plays guitar up on stage. I stand up and clap along, since to do otherwise would make me more conspicuous. I sing about love and faith and joy and think, I'd trade all this for a nice salutary dose of hell. Sanitised religion is despicable. Humans want to be punished when they've transgressed, not all this endless beaming love, not unless they're bloody retarded. They want to undergo the transformative power of suffering. A good domme could accomplish it in half an hour, and charge an awful lot less. But then, I suspect cruelty and pain wouldn't appeal to such great swathes of humanity had they not been corrupted by Christianity.

Old school Greek and Roman Gods also inflicted suffering, but with them it was indiscriminate, random, cruel and capricious. The masterstroke of Christianity – the reason it's survived as long as it has – is the way it gives misery meaning. The Buddhists have spotted that too. To live is to suffer, to survive is to find meaning in the suffering, all that stuff. Pure suffering, without a hint of resentment or pride to it: suffering undergone joyously, in a spirit of hope and repentance: that's the kind of suffering that will transform. A suffering mingled with love and gratitude, whether for God or your Mistress, I don't think it much matters, and that's why I'll burn.

Any other kind, incidentally, will corrupt. Abused children are unlikely to grow up angelic. When life is predicated upon survival rather than tenderness it tends to skew your moral compass. Instead your philosophy tends towards - get what you want, by any means, only don't get caught.

So one's mind wanders, in among the tambourines. I can get caught up in the collective joy, but today it merely irritates. Did they really believe all this stuff? And if they did why the devil couldn't they believe it quietly?

Robert had been treating me very kindly, as though I were recuperating from flu. So far I had managed to be nice to him, hide my thriving business and continue to see punters at Katie's while she was at work, leaving the odd bottle of wine as recompense, and writing her some personalised erotica about her being my darling breastfed little baby who needed a very good scrub down in the bath, followed by a jolly good spanking for being bad and splashing mummy. I didn't particularly miss the Katie chapter, but it still hurt that she'd decided to chuck me out and try something new.

So anyway that was all fine, as fine as it gets, a good stable home and work life, like the magazines recommend. And then this man kept messaging me. It had been going on about a fortnight now. He'd spotted my legs on Instagram, probably. #nylons. To this much I was accustomed. But this man was being vaguely interesting, even when I was sober, which was different and new. He messaged not to tell me he wanted to get to know me better, or if I could send him something slightly saucier. No: he wrote to tell me he forgave me. *I see you and I forgive you.* That was all. In my current. confused, slightly nervy state, this seemed to have some significance I couldn't quite fathom. *I see you and I forgive you.* And later: *Guilt is useless. I know all and I forgive you. In Christ's name.*

The fact he was aligning himself with Christ sounded a warning bell, but I was bored and curious, and I bit back.

Forgive me for what?

Eight hours passed before he answered. The waiting was intriguing. Usually I make them wait. Waiting is a powerful punishment.

Finally: *You know what.*

So that was totally worth waiting for. And a few hours after that: *I'm a very forgiving person. The only human I cannot forgive is myself.*

Big bollocking deal. But Robert's snoring reverberated angrily through the wall, I'd played all my scrabble games, my mind still whirred like a spin dryer, so I stared into the darkness and wondered about responding. It was doubtless a punter who'd figured out my real name and was enjoying tormenting me. I'm not as careful to conceal my identity as I could be. Nothing scarier than a snubbed sub. I shouldn't answer. Still.

What did you do?

He read it alright, but didn't reply. Fine. Bugger you then. I opened his profile, resenting the curiosity he'd quickened. He appeared to be the kind of moody, melancholy creature for whom women can quickly feel pity, which, if not checked, can turn to love, like snow to shitty sleet, and that was the last damn thing I needed. His profile picture showed a doleful, soulful creature, not unattractive. His photographs were of mountains and sparrows, not a single human being among them, and, I noticed, with a barely suppressed tut, barely a hashtag. Didn't he want to be liked? Good photographs, some of them, even I could see that, not that it much mattered, but garnering one or two likes at best. Pathetic. Perhaps his crapness at social media was what needed forgiving. No second chances here, pal. I tutted louder at the ineptitude.

Can you help me?

Oh here we go. And yet–

What help do you need?

Silence again. I wondered vaguely if he might kill himself, and if so, what I could do about it. I'd no idea where in the world he was, bugger all I could do, and yet I'd feel guilty all the same. How bloody irritating.

I don't know. I DON'T KNOW.

Well I sure as shit don't. Why pick on me?

Silence. I sighed.

You're not going to top yourself, are you?

No.

Thank God for that.

I haven't the guts.

Couldn't think how to answer that. Jolly good? Have you tried cracking one off? Be the change you want to see in the world? Received wisdom would be to drop some platitude like, it takes more courage to live, but that was patently nonsense. To take no action, to keep doing what you've always done, takes no courage at all.

I snuck another look at his picture. Big brown eyes, dark hair, probably mid-forties. Classic midlife crisis territory. Probably divorced, with a couple of kids he'd begun to bore.

There's nothing for me but to wait for death. Suicide isn't an option. Do you understand?

I understand the words, but not the concept. There's lots to do. Money to make. And don't you have any enemies you want to infuriate?

Plenty of enemies. But why would I care to hurt them?

Oh well. Find another hobby then. Find meaning in the suffering. There aren't any other possibilities.

A pause. And then: *What's your meaning?*

Next day, grumpy, bleary-eyed, I went with Robert to visit his parents, who were as thrilled to have me back as he was.

Clearly he hadn't tried to explain the flatmate concept. I'd assumed they would hate me, but they couldn't help but be overjoyed at seeing Rob smile again. Only child, you know. I found myself slipping back into the old patterns, acting the part of Rob's devoted wife. They asked after Beth and my health and holiday plans, my cunning little handbag, what I was reading. We ate lunch to the accompaniment of a loudly ticking clock, perched on tall chairs which forced you upright. Lamb and greens, a jug of oily water. Robert's mother told me anecdotes about next door's naughty poodle, while Robert was gently berated for his inability to ensure a regular income. We all pretended that earning a living was beneath me; the mere notion of Rob's wife needing money was offensive. It's so soothing, being what people expect, sliding straight into the grooves they carved out decades before. No phones at table, of course, but my back pocket gently buzzed throughout, sending jolts through my spine, like lust, or the prick of a conscience.

Chapter Nine

I spent a week being unemployed. It was heavenly. I caught up with friends, moved from an itchy bedsit in East Acton to a fabulous vegan house share in Camberwell, a flock of geese in the back garden and a Buddha beaming at me from every room. A teacher and a care-home manager lived there already, and seemed curiously unmoved when I described myself as an unemployed dancer. I was confident I wouldn't be unemployed for long, anyway. I was 19, and more than happy to get my tits out, and during my four months at the Windmill I had found these were highly marketable assets.

Or I could, of course, get a proper job. I could work for that nice, independent wine seller, for instance. I considered it, I honestly did. But it all seemed a bit tricky, trying to make a good impression while leaving my tights on. I was still pondering what to do when I walked down Brewer Street one day to meet my sort of boyfriend for lunch. I was looking about me, as one might well do, at all the wonderful sights: the porn shops, the Raymond Revue Bar, handwritten signs and bits of cardboard telling of lingerie models. (You know, sometimes these girls really are lingerie models. That's the scam. A chap walks up a staircase expecting a shag, and finds a girl posing in a variety of knickers: if he suggests they take it further, a big beefy chap suddenly appears, explains the experience has already cost £100, and frog marches him to a cashpoint. But I digress.)

And the peepshows, of course: 'Naked girls for £2' screamed the signs. Grumpy looking girls stood outside these places, presumably having been instructed to look enticing five hours earlier. Outside one stood a rather handsome man, who smiled when he saw me looking.

"Would you like a job?"

Never one to ignore the hand of fate, I smiled back.

"Yes please!"

"Dancing or Hostessing?"

"Dancing," I said firmly. I never wanted to speak to another heterosexual man again for as long as I lived, into which category this chap happily didn't fall.

"There's more money in Hostessing."

"Never mind."

"And you speak such good English too. What a waste. Well, we'll start you in the peep slots then. Wanna come see?"

I followed him into the tiny shop. To the customer it looked like a row of four sunbathing cubicles on a mucky carpet. Walk through the door marked 'Staff' however, and you'd find two girls sitting in their pants. One, who had a punter, was twirling round a pole. The other was reading *Pride and Prejudice*.

"So it's one girl to two slots? What if you get two fellas at once?"

"Just make sure you smile, and look at both of them. See, now–"

There was a sudden rattling, and another letterbox slot fell open in the cubicle of the girl already dancing. Two pairs of eyes were now following her cavortings. Without missing a beat, she draped her snatch over one slot, while pressing her tits against the other. In this position, her face was her own: she looked up and winked at me.

"Start tomorrow?" the fella suggested. "Eleven till five, £40 a shift. If you're popular we'll get you some more shifts. Trial run, ok? Bring a picnic!"

"And a book," muttered the less popular girl, sitting forlorn as her colleague sweated and pranced.

Well, I had nothing else to do, so I went along and found it was all good fun, really. It certainly cut down on all that irritating social interaction I'd found so debilitating at the

Windmill. You sat in your cubicle, about the size of a disabled loo, separated from your co-worker by a pink curtain. In your workspace was a shelf and a pole. You could sit on the shelf and hide your bottle of wine beneath it, and use it to steady yourself on the pole when you had a customer.

Ostensibly, you were supposed to perform a strip show, but as £2 only bought the gentleman a minute of your time, there wasn't really much chance to piss about with boas and tassels. You could either sit about all day in your bra, or in your pants, so that you'd have just one garment to remove when a slot came down. I sat about in my bra. I've always been slightly self-conscious about my tits – they're not uniform shape or size, and I feel I need to tweak my nipples incessantly to get them looking pointy and perky. A minge is a minge, so I elected to keep that on show.

When a slot slammed down, you could only see a pair of eyes, and you could scarcely make out if you were being watched by someone young or old, black or white, male or female. Not that it much mattered. It was just weird, that's all, though I guess not much weirder than being on a lit stage looking out to a dark auditorium, not knowing who was looking. The intense intimacy made it seem weirder though. You'd press your groin near their hole, and hear them wanking. Occasionally they would lift a finger to the slot and swivel it, indicating that they'd like you to turn round and show your arse. One chap, who turned up most days, would make a strange jingling noise as he tossed himself off, the result of several genital piercings and a handsome collection of signet rings, according to my boss, Mario. A rhythmic 'jingle, jingle, jingle' as I danced, like sleigh bells. When the other girl went to the loo, you could bet your bloody life all four slots would open at once, so you'd have to charge back and forth between them, pressing your crotch frantically against one window, then another, desperately trying to ensure each customer got his £2 worth of minge.

I was fairly popular. I could tuck one leg behind my ear, and show them a split beaver all the way to my cervix, one presumes.

I got given shifts three or four times a week, but I was still on the lookout for something more full time. After a steady grand a week, the money seemed utterly crap. And Mario kept scheduling my shifts to coincide with those of a German girl, who rather smelled, smoked incessantly and talked all day about how much she hated the Jews. To no avail did I sit pointedly reading the *Guardian*, or suggest that she move away from Golders Green: no, this was her sole conversational topic, how the Jews were taking over and conspiring against us. It quickly became wearing.

I decided to look more strenuously elsewhere for employment. But it was interesting while it lasted. I wonder if that beautiful German girl is still sitting there, day after day, chain smoking, cursing the Jews and showing her strangely rubbery flange, running outside every time her boyfriend rang to maintain the fiction that she worked in a clothes shop? I suppose not. Yet she seemed so much a part of the experience I can hardly imagine it without her.

I don't want you to imagine I spent all my time wandering about Soho looking round brothels and their attendant businesses, and yet that was how I found my third job. I'd acquired a new boyfriend who worked at Centrepoint, with a mania for vegan wholefood lunches – unusual in a man, and probably unique in a Scotsman. We'd go for mung bean salads at Mildred's on Wardour Street, and I'd try to decide whether I liked him or not, and if the mung beans somehow compensated for the huge quantity of beer he managed to swallow alongside them.

On one of these occasions I chose to walk to the tube via Dean Street and stood gawping before the Sunset Strip theatre. It had three notices in the window ('New to Soho, Blue Pole Dancing!', 'Totally Nude Dancers!' and, smaller and more prosaic, 'Girls Wanted'). I pondered whether to wander in and enquire. Thank God I did. This marked the beginning of two of the happiest years of my life.

The Sunset Strip was run by Freddie, an elderly, twinkly old man, white haired and dapper, who managed to be charming and respectful, while managing one of the most successful businesses in Soho. He saw me looking in, and gave a little wave from behind his desk, where he sat surrounded by pictures of semi-clad girls from the last five decades, all beaming stoically.

"Hello darling, can I help?"

"Well, I saw your notice in the window, about wanting girls…"

"Ah yes?" He ran a glance over my figure. I was in jeans and a t-shirt, topped fetchingly with a fawn anorak.

"Would you like to audition now, dear? I'm sure we could squeeze you in somewhere…"

He ran a finger down a photocopied sheet, which read: '2.10 Juliet 2.20 Louise 2.30 Nina…' and so on, all the way down to 9 p.m.

"You can take Juliet's dance in ten minutes time, perhaps. She's been moaning about her knee all morning…"

"Oh! Really? Now? But…" – I looked down in panic at my jeans – "I haven't got any stuff. Clothes. And I've never danced for ten minutes before…"

"You'll be fine, darling. It's only eight minutes really. We allow two minutes in between acts to reset the stage. And it's just wiggling. Just wiggle. The girls will sort you out." He reached forward and spoke into an old-fashioned intercom system.

"Girls! We've got an auditionee here. Can someone come and get her and kit here out for the 2.10 show?"

A short pause, then a thick foreign accent crackled back to us.

"Freddie, is Nina. Coming now."

The moment she'd finished speaking, it seemed, a partially concealed door in the corner opened, and a tall, dark, clearly naked girl poked most of her torso round the corner, and winked at me.

"Hallo, Hallo! This way please…"

Baffled by the sudden turn of events, I followed her down a murky little corridor, barely lit by a dim, solitary bulb. After the bright sunshine, it was like entering a dungeon.

"You dance before?"

"Ah, well, a bit. At the Windmill, you know?... Just down the road?"

"Ah, Windmill are bastards. You were fired?"

"Well, no..." She looked disappointed, so I added "I just walked out! Ha! Owe them money and everything!"

If she was impressed by my latent criminal streak, she hid it well.

"You have clothes, music?"

"No, this is all a bit unexpected really–"

"Don't matter, you wear one of mine." And she opened another tiny door to reveal a dressing room, crammed to the rafters with girls, sequins, boas and smoke. It looked like the tiniest, most over-stuffed knick-knack shop in the world. Seven girls, in a room perhaps seven feet square, each with nine costume changes and a day's worth of paraphernalia – books, tuna salad, wine, shoes, phones, makeup. It was bedlam. They all looked up at me and murmured a greeting. I shuffled my feet and tried to avert my gaze. Walking into a room of mainly naked strangers never stops feeling odd. And now Nina was starting to remove my clothes and hold up an assortment of her own clothes against my shabby underwear, to decide which would do me most good.

"We must be quick, yes? You are on in five minutes."

"Oh, Christ, I–"

"Your bra is horrid. Best take it off. Knickers will do."

Fortunately, I'd put on a black lacy bikini pair this morning, boring, but passable. My mother isn't the type to warn me about always wearing clean, intact underwear in case of a car crash, otherwise she'd feel fully entitled to gloat at this experience.

"This dress is good on you. You will wear this."

A tight, purple, clingy halter neck: it showed off my legs, and skimmed over my pudgy belly with surprising efficiency.

"What shoe size?"

"Um. Seven."

"Me too. You will wear these."

She kicked off her stilettos, and supported me as I pushed my own sweaty toes into them. I made a mental note to thank her when I was feeling less hysterical.

"You have a garter?" Another girl had popped up beside me, grabbing my arm as I wobbled. In truth, my shoe size is closer to eight than seven, and I'm hopeless at dancing in towering heels anyway. Seeing my bewilderment, she lifted her skirt.

"You know, garter belt? For tips?" She twanged at a pretty white lace affair.

"Oh, no. I don't. Is that how it works?"

"Uh-huh." She pulled it off her leg and thrust it onto mine. I'd never been touched by so many people at once: it was like a porn film. Another girl was smoothing down my hair now, while another, possibly her twin, was brushing glitter into my décolletage.

"You like Prince?" Nina said encouragingly, as if to a simpleton. "Maybe 'Horny Pony'?" She pronounced it as 'Hhherrrnee Perny'.

"Um. Sure, why not?" At least being at the Windmill had taught me not to be precious about the music I used. Anything with a beat suited me. I could hear a muted ripple of applause from somewhere not too far away, followed by a rather louder squeaking.

"That's curtains," said Nina. "It is your turn. You are ready? We go down now. Here is Jessica." I heard a stomp, stomp, stomp up some stairs, interspersed with some heavy breathing and the occasional curse. A skinny dark girl smashed into the room, throwing a pile of clothes, then herself, into a chair, all while shaking her head theatrically at her reflection.

"Today is not so good for the tips. It is a good day to try out new things," said Nina, philosophically.

"But – but – what do I do?" I said in despair, as she started to lead me back out into the corridor, down some still murkier steps, covered treacherously in all manner of detritus.

"First song, take clothes off. Second song, dance about. Easy. Here is John. 'Horny Pony' John. See you soon. Good luck!" And she darted away, my newly found saviour, now truly totally naked, as I'd even taken the shoes from her feet.

John was a sweet, elderly, dithering man who sat all day in a cupboard filled with thousands upon thousands of cassette tapes, all labelled in tiny handwriting. This, then, was the DJ. Not quite so flash as at the Windmill, but he gave me a friendly nod as he found the song and pointed me to the stage.

"You get a prop if you want. Bed or chair?"

"Chair," I said, firmly. I'd some experience of incorporating a chair into my act: a bed sounded horrifying. He fetched it for me.

"There you are then, sweetheart. Off you go. Good luck."

And so, only ten minutes after I'd been walking along a sunny street with scarcely a care in the world, I found myself standing alone on a small stage, surrounded by thick red curtains, in an assortment of mismatched, ill-fitting clothes, listening to the coughs and mutterings of an audience I couldn't see, who'd paid money to be entertained: an entertainment I would now have to supply for eight, long, bloody minutes. The curtains began to squeak, and part. I arranged my face into something like a smile, and decided at the last minute to drape myself over the chair, *Cabaret* style, which won me a little bemused clapping on the reveal. I didn't dare look at my audience, not yet. Instead I began to run my hands over my body, in a mock wanky style that had served me quite well at the Windmill. I got more applause! There was actual mid-dance clapping for this nonsense, and a few cries of "Jolly good!" and "More!" Encouraged, I took a peek. And saw a proper auditorium, though small, with about 50 or 60 red velvet chairs, half of them filled with men. Not Windmill men, these, but older men, quite a few pensioners, not a suit in sight. Although – what else could you expect on a Tuesday afternoon? Still, it was depressing to see that a couple of them were asleep. I continued to wiggle. There were two poles here, right on the edge of the stage, so you could sweep your buttocks an inch from the audiences faces, if you fancied.

I had a little exploratory twirl. One of the more vocal men took this opportunity to grab at my thigh; I considered stabbing him in the face with my stiletto, but spotted the old man from upstairs standing at the back, watching me, and thought I'd best bide my time. God, how long was eight minutes anyway? At least here there were three distinct bits of audience to dance to, whereas at the Windmill you either had several dots in the distance, or one man, who had probably seen enough of your tits and flange after a minute or so, but felt awkward about heading back to the bar.

The pensioners were still roaring their approval, and Gropey had another little go at my thigh. I felt that I couldn't really let this go unpunished, so I waggled my finger admonishingly at him. He blushed.

"I'm sorry, I couldn't help it…" he murmured, and slumped back into his seat, crushed.

Wearing so few clothes made life tricky. I'd lost the dress and pants within 30 seconds, and found myself with another six minutes to fill with naked cavorting. Not knowing the songs, I had no idea how long I had been on for, and thought it impolite – nay, a deal breaker – to look at my watch. I decided to lie down on the floor, as my shoes were pinching. Huge round of applause. There can't be many jobs where giving up and lying down earns you an ovation.

Finally the noise stopped, the clapping reached a peak, and the curtain squeaked shut. Slowly, I rose to my feet, found Nina's now rather sweaty dress, and clambered heavily back up the stairs. I was out of shape. That would have to change.

The other girls were all hanging round in the corridor, looking rather sheepish, as if they'd all been peeping round the curtain at me, and only just got back in time. I handed Nina back her dress.

"Thank you so much!"

"Alright? How much did you get?"

"Get? Oh, nothing." That couldn't be good.

"What's this then?" said the tall blonde, flicking a finger under her garter belt. A little shower of pound coins fell out.

That darling pensioner had been trying to tip me, not grope me! I picked them up. Four pound coins.

"Do I get to keep them?" I asked, in wonderment.

"Of course. £35 a day wages, plus all your tips."

It wasn't Windmill money, but it was a damn sight easier to come by, and the girls all looked so encouraging and pleased for me that I felt almost tearful. I climbed back into my jeans and went back upstairs to hear my fate. It would be too awful to go through all that just to get rejected, with only my tube fare to show for it. I went out to see the old boy, pink faced and white haired, beaming at me like a jolly elf.

"Alright darling? Could you start tomorrow?"

Chapter Ten

One dull evening I clambered back into the marital bed, a moment of madness born more of masochism than lust. There's something soothing about a husband of one's own. You know how best to curl about them, in bed and through the days. I slid straight back into the same old routine, being brought tea in bed, big shop in Tesco of a Thursday, the endless perky lying. He hadn't filled the dusty holes where my possessions used to live, so that they slid straight back into place too. The lamps and saucers we'd chosen together, tragic and incongruous when bereft of their proper purpose, seemed to cheer up, become perky and gay, as indeed did I. Rob was so happy to find that I was happy, that the new rules and existence had made me happier than ever, that he became happier than ever, and on and on, a virtuous circle, turning on tracks of duplicity, all aboard the smile train.

I wallowed in an urge to placate him and submit, thrilling and erotic in the abstract. For the moment, back home, moving between our accustomed dents in sofa and bed, he seemed ecstatic, and it felt churlish to spoil his happiness with my misgivings. I'm made to vacillate between teasing and submitting. Probably my only true chance of happiness lies in total submission, which is presumably why I resist it so powerfully. Like the addicts who publicly confess their inability to master their own lives, I decided to make Robert my higher power, follow his bidding, surrender thought and replace it with devotion.

Which all sounds very fine in theory. But sadly there was nothing much Godlike about Robert. I watched him drive away in his battered van the morning after our passionate, drunken reconciliation, whistling noisily, stopping at the end of the road to post a letter. He pulled up by the post box and wound down his window, couldn't quite reach, so reversed back up a little; still couldn't make it, so moved forward, then back, until finally, with an audible groan, managing to extend his chewed fingertips to the slit, before bouncing round the corner. I'd probably have three hours while he went through his band meeting and practise. Time enough for a shibari session. My whole being ached to pick up my phone and make it happen. A creative giddy afternoon with a chum and £300. Instead I stuffed said phone in a drawer, under my long neglected gym outfits, and went to make a pie. There's a satisfaction in rolling out pastry. It yields a similar throb in the biceps as wielding a cane, while the neat patterns and markings are also hazily reminiscent. The radio played and the sun warmed my back. It wouldn't last, but I could enjoy today. I stabbed at my pastry. Donald was in London this week. Champagne, 200 strokes of the cane, thick wad of notes in a Basildon Bond envelope, passed to me with a bow and a whispered, "Your honorarium, Madam."

I didn't even like champagne, damn it. I sliced mushrooms and onions, set them sizzling with wine and cream. The kitchen smelled delicious. Rob's plan was that I should live on my savings while I "looked around for something suitable." I came from proper Dickensian poverty and feared its return more than I feared death. Robert laughed at my agonising over an extra 10 p for a fancier loaf of bread, but I knew that amnesia to privilege tends to precipitate its loss, and he, the posh sap, did not. I quite fancied being a hospital porter, although I felt nervous about admitting it, with that idiotic degree weighing me down: good exercise and interesting anecdotes. Hospitals make me feel safe, probably their proximity to danger and death.

There was talk of my getting back into singing, too. In his band. Support him. And get them more gigs and all that, since I've such a knack for drumming up trade, ha bloody ha. I wasn't exactly brimming with joy at that plan, although I acted like I was. But I don't do well playing second fiddle, which in this instance I almost literally would be. I needed something which was mine. Robert suggested I throw myself into mothering, at which I badly stifled a snort. Nineteen-year-old girls need less mothering, not more, and Beth less than most. She's studying political history in Leicester now, full of plans to improve the world, dear idiot child. I took an off-shoot of pastry and made a second, smaller, low-fat vegan version. Took pleasure crimping the edges in perfect symmetry.

It's easier for a domme to submit than you might think. She understands exactly what submission involves. It's not about being powerless, but surrendering your power to the one you deem most worthy of wielding it. Which, in all good conscience, I couldn't believe was Robert. Robert was the thing I couldn't change as well as the thing I could, and I'd need to find the courage and wisdom to manage both.

There's an ecstasy in surrender, and I yielded to it like the vicious little slut I am. Handed him the black book which detailed all the punters' names, numbers, grandkids' names, how they took their tea, variant sexual preferences: a blackmailer's wet dream. I broke my canes before him, which is trickier than it sounds – the beasts are built to yield under pressure, not break; a salutary lesson to all of us. I tucked away the silk blouses and pencil skirts he so detested, reverted to boots, jeans and band shirts. It still felt like dressing up, but this time only to please one man, the man, the man who is the measure of all things. I shopped and cleaned. When the punters wrote wanting sessions, I told them I'd retired. They were suitably dismayed and I wallowed in my martyrdom, sucked on it like a lozenge.

Friend of mine, raised a Jehovah's Witness, told me once how she decided to kill herself at 16 when she knew for sure she was a lesbian. She couldn't bear the idea of losing her family's love and disappointing Jesus. And I made suitably sympathetic noises, of course, but really I thought: you arrogant, tedious cow, what astonishing hubris. Imagine actually believing Jesus cares what you do with your smelly bits. Sure, Jesus could be busy worried about world peace, world hunger, kids with cancer, but instead you think it likelier he worries whether it's Jim or Jane finger-banging you, the kinky thorn-riddled beggar. I credit Jesus with more sense than that, and I don't call myself a Christian. But you have to admit Jesus said some sensible stuff: love your neighbour, be grateful for what you've got, act nice to whores, their feet bloody well hurt and stink from being encased in rubber boots all day, give 'em a rub and a wink.

Jesus, like Socrates and Buddha, never bothered writing anything down though, did he? So I guess we can't be sure he doesn't worry about scissoring more than genocide. Like I say, sensible chap: writing's hard. But the moody Jesus type who'd been writing to me had been writing more, largely exploring some esoteric weird misery of his I could never fully fathom – either his meaning or my interest in it. He seemed to be an artist, and like most of them, hounded by some artistic failure, a sense his great talent wasn't taken seriously enough, blah. Then it started to get more interesting.

Some of your pictures are pretty good.

Now that's more like it. Bit off-hand, not nearly obsequious enough, but much more my level, all the same.

But I don't think they capture your true beauty.

There's sod all beauty to me, pal. I'm in my 40s, a stone overweight, I drink too much, my gut and tits sag from a massive baby-making bonanza. Beauty's long departed.

Yes. I see all that.

Christ. Are you single, by any chance?

No. But it's not about parts of the body. If they're flabby or scarred or wrinkled. That doesn't matter. It's about having the confidence to show defects that creates the power of the image. Perfection is boring. Courage, never. Do you see?

I stared at my phone. I did see. And my initial instinct to type, furiously, look, mate, if you want to see my tits I can send you straight to my Onlyfans, withered on my fingertips. Instead:

You talk a lot about portrait photography for someone who specialises in swans and squirrels.

I do humans too. I exhibit occasionally. I don't squander models' work on social media.

Why?

Silence. Bastard.

Look, it's advertising for me. Free marketing, a place to display my wares. My body is my business. I sell my flesh and its promises. Instagram is my shop window.

You could model for me.

Oh, could I? Gee, thanks.

There's an interesting quality to your face.

Which you can only capture by stripping me naked, no doubt. So you're married?

I am. So are you.

Well. Yes.

Your husband adores you. He's always tagging you in to family photos, his arm round you, beaming away. He can't believe his luck. Rightly, I suspect.

He appreciates what he has, it's true.

What he imagines he has. Meet me at St Agatha's Church at 8 am next Thursday.

Mate. I'm not 12. I'm not meeting a random stranger who's contacted me on social.

But you must. All the time. For your work.

That's different. There are boundaries in place. Procedures. They want a caning: I ask £100 an hour: if they've got it they come to my house and get a caning, and if I don't know them my mum hides upstairs with a mace spray and baseball bat. Simple. I don't meet them in churches.

I've no interest in caning.

Sure? Might cheer you up. Been used to treat depression in Russia and the like.

I don't need to be cheered up. I need forgiveness.

Oh Christ, not this again. For what, raping and murdering whores in church doorways? And you think photographing me will help?

Unlikely. But it may banish misery for a few hours.

Well that sounds a right treat for me. Why a church? To aid with the forgiveness quest?

I like churches. Don't you? Quiet, thoughtful. Nice public places. You might be a lunatic, after all.

Fair point. I'll think about it and let you know.

You'll come.

I'll have to tell hubby I've taken up jogging…

But he was gone. I fought down rage at the knowledge he was right. I would go to a church and meet a stranger because he'd told me to. My urge to obey, to please, overcame all else. And if I didn't go I suspected I wouldn't hear from him again.

Chapter Eleven

The best thing about the Sunset Strip? It was almost like having a proper job. Five mornings a week I turned up at 10.45 a.m., and was let out to go home around 8 p.m. In the middle, I gave seven or eight shows, depending on how many girls were working, for which I earned £5 each: with tips, I earned a steady £70 to £80 a day, sometimes more. And when I wasn't dancing, my time was my own. I could put my clothes back on, go out on to Oxford Street for coffee, browse the shops, hit the pub; or, I could stay in that small, smoky dressing room and read my book. Freddie didn't give a damn what you did as long as you were on stage at the prescribed time. Every morning he would laboriously scrawl a timetable with our names in strict rotation from 11 a.m. till 8 p.m. hiding his handiwork whenever a punter came in. At 12 he'd finally finish it, calling through for one of us to collect it, hissing a warning if he saw a man glancing in its direction. He was an absolute darling, fiercely loyal and protective of us, and utterly dismissive of his clientele.

One afternoon a boy who who'd sat next to me in maths class five years ago recognised me from a poster outside, and tried to storm past reception to find me for a bit of a chat: Freddie knocked him sideways and sat on him, then calmly rang through to ask me to pop out to identify 'a certain gentleman' who claimed 'a prior knowledge' of me. Freddie also gave us £40 a week for drink, with which we bought value vodka and Coca Cola from the local Somerfield. On hot summer days, we were sent to buy ice cream too, packets of magnums which he would dispense to us, twinkly and excited at our gratitude.

It was like working for Father Christmas, apart from the pole-dancing and 'total' nudity.

And I found I quite enjoyed giving these shows. Eight minutes was long enough to give an interesting, creative performance, and I started to put some thought into my costumes and music. I was expected to have a few different outfits, so spent a few hours scouring charity shops for sequins, gauze, feathers. Encouraged to be different, to expand as a performer, I started dancing to the music I loved – Nina Simone, Billie Holiday, Dinah Washington – and quickly became known as the classy, serious one. I played on this theme, choosing outfits which were elegant and timeless, lots of long, dragging hems with slits up the side, sparkly shoes, hats.

I was so healthy and happy I was almost unbearable. I worked with a nice bunch of girls, the usual mix of students, travellers and mothers, not nearly so hardened as those at the Windmill: we weren't fighting each other for an income, so we could afford to be friends. Oh, the stories I heard! But these aren't my stories, and I can't repeat them – much. I remember a girl of gypsy origin, who had no idea of when her birthday was or how old she might be. A girl who'd trained at the Royal Ballet. A girl who'd performed at the weirdest of fetish clubs, could breathe fire from her snatch, and had to be discouraged from peeing on stage. The girl who claimed to be a 200-year-old vampire, and used a bottle of fake blood a day on stage, covering tampons in it and claiming to use them as teabags: ('Keeps me young, dahlings…') There were prostitutes down on their luck, fired from their agencies and comparing notes, a PhD student writing a thesis on comparative religion; three Spanish sisters whom I never learnt to tell apart, and even one poor, pale soul who worked at the Sunset 11 a.m. till 8 p.m., then trotted off to the Windmill to work from 8.30 p.m. until 3.30 a.m. She slept in the corridor between her dances, and had to be woken and reminded to dance and eat.

It was all such fun! It sounds ridiculous, but it gave me routine and stability, which my previous life had lacked.

I dropped the pretence that I was going back to Oxford to complete my degree, and stayed on for two and a half years. I might never have left, if only Freddie hadn't been bought out and dismissed.

Each morning I rose early and took two aerobics classes at the local gym, before taking the tube into Soho. Usually I had lunch with my bloke at some point, and the evenings were devoted to drinking. It was a pleasant, mindless existence. Eventually I decided to go to Birkbeck to take a part-time English degree, feeling vaguely guilty that my brain must be atrophying. I read the books and wrote the essays sitting in my pants and heels, while around me half naked girls took drugs, had hysterics, worried about their children, debts, futures, sewed on sequins, checked their stocks and shares, or wrote their essays alongside me. It was chaos, but organised chaos, and it suited me. And all the time I learned more and more about the flesh trade from all those wonderful girls' stories.

When I look back now, every day seems like it was perfect, golden, full of fun, like the way you're meant to remember your childhood as always sunny. There must have been some crappy days. I remember one girl showing up who was rumoured to steal, which led to a lot of unpleasant accusations and screaming, a dustpan and brush being thrown and a few bitch slaps. I went down the road for a pint, and when I came back, she'd gone. So that was fine. The Spanish sisters used to have awful, physical fights too, on occasion: I tried to intervene once, when one started to pour boiling water over another, but generally I left them to it. They could be gouging out each other's eyes one minute, and making up the next.

I started to get a few regulars, whom I could depend on for tips, and occasionally presents. Most weeks I would receive a bunch of flowers, four or five boxes of chocolates, some lousy poetry. A tramp used to lurk outside the Sunset at closing time, and we'd give most of the chocolate to him – we'd have been 20 stone, and toothless if we hadn't. I kept some of the poetry, like this delightful offering:

You were so obviously new
The first time that I saw you
So gloriously young and fresh
That I, hopeful of a chance
To brush your luscious flesh
Proffered a perverted fiver
Your private dance to letch
So near, and yet so far
Your silky soft vagina
Fluttered before my eyes
As I sat mesmerised
By the ecstasy of your thighs
To boldly go
From Oxford down to Soho
Armed only with your genitalia
So straddling the social high and low
Reveals your breadth of character
To get such satisfaction
In making so very happy
Lonely men like me,
Shows a warmth of vision
Which many cannot see
You became a stripper
To ease the Oxbridge pressure
Now you have given so much pleasure
And voyeuristic relief
Give yourself, self-belief
You know there's more to you
Than your excellent essays on Rousseau,
Or men, with a mentality you eschew,
Viewing you, as just a screw,
You're unique, precious, only you.
I am sure, in the fullness of time,
You will find men wanting the beauty of your mind.
And with the arrival of real love,
Your confusion will come to cease

Relieved by the true satisfaction of peace.

One drizzly morning in June I turned up to work to find a little cluster of girls, miserable and idle, on the pavement outside. Usually we were all very keen to duck in as fast as possible, away from curious eyes, so this seemed extraordinary. I looked at Nina, who'd been there ten years and usually took charge in a crisis.

"Has Freddy not shown up?"

"No, he here alright." She made a low guttural growl of disgust deep in her throat. "Stupid bastard bloody bitch feminists glued up the locks. We can't get in. He's gone to borrow tools."

"Oh, shit."

"Yes. Exactly. Shit."

Around us Soho was starting to come to life. A few chaps I was pretty sure I recognised as punters were ducking past the Sunset and hurrying along to a club a few doors down instead, trying their best not to make eye contact with any of us.

"They left a note on the door saying 'Respect Women'," said Juliet. "But how is this respecting women exactly? People are staring and laughing at us. And how am I going to pay my childminder?"

There was a lot of nodding at this. The feminists didn't sign up many recruits that day. Freddy couldn't open the locks for us, so we all had to take the day off. The punters couldn't have cared less; they were surrounded by minge anyway. Freddie was rich enough to be quite pleased by the unexpected holiday. But the girls with children were screwed. Some didn't even have enough money to get the tube home. After a moment's hesitation, Freddie nipped off to the cashpoint so he could give us all a day's wages, rolling his eyes, embarrassed, at our gratitude. Juliet was ecstatic, crying on his chest. The rain cleared up, so I walked the eight miles back to my flat in North London, spending much of the time worrying about what I'd do when I was too old to strip. I was 21, and knew I couldn't go on beyond 30 without getting the piss ripped out of me by girls and punters alike. But still, I'd have my degree by then, and everyone knew what an economic powerhouse an English graduate could be.

At home I relished the pleasure of keeping my pants on all day, cleaned my skanky flat, and made vegetable lasagne and apple crumble, much to my boyfriend's astonishment, largely to piss off the feminists. Force me out of the workplace and into the kitchen, will you, you raging great bourgeois eejits?

On election day 1997 we made a banner for the stage, which read 'The Girls of the Sunset Strip support Tony Blair'. We wore red all day long, and danced to 'Things Can Only Get Better' until Freddie begged us to stop. Most of the girls weren't even registered to vote, but we all wanted to do our bit anyway. And we were all tipped handsomely by the crowd for combining political awareness with nudity. New Labour certainly seemed to promise a brighter future for the whores.

There were very few English girls at the Sunset. Most of the time it was just the ballerina and me. But our numbers were swelled one afternoon, doubled in fact, when a beautiful blonde arrived, grinning hugely, and very obviously pregnant.

Men love the pregnant girls. Jade earned three times as much as any of us, but she was too sweet for us to resent her, although we were all pretty glad she and bump would have to push off in a month or two. Her husband was in prison, so she was on her own for the next four years, and pretty much homeless, sleeping on a friend's sofa, and stretching their friendship to the limit. She'd saved enough money to rent a flat, but with no references, pay slips or bank account, and only a swollen belly to her name, no one was prepared to take a chance on her. She'd been to the council to get a flat, but was told she would only be housed by the time the baby was due if she were a battered wife. She told me all this one morning while I was applying my makeup, then sat back and looked at me expectantly. I tutted with genuine sympathy, although half my mind was occupied with worrying about how best to remove my leopard print thong without the crusty bits showing. I was always too drunk at the end of the night to remember to take my pants home for a wash.

"So could you help me?"

"Eh? Oh, well, I'd love to, of course. But how?"

"Beat me up!"

"Oh, piss off. I'm not beating up a heavily pregnant woman. My karma's already shafted." I looked at her. "Why me, anyway?"

"Oh, I don't know… just because you're always so quiet I thought you might have a latent psychotic streak, I suppose."

"Oh, cheers. No, that's just me being slightly shy, rather than plotting atrocities. You dope."

"Sorry."

"I should bloody well think so." She looked sorry, and utterly woebegone. "Look, do you want me to go round flats pretending to be you? I've got a bank account, no bun in my oven, and people tend to do as I say when they hear my accent."

She brightened. "Oh, would you? That'd be brilliant!"

In the end, though, she decided it would be easier to get beaten up, council rents being so much cheaper. I had to leave the room while it was happening, but a couple of the girls seemed awfully keen. Maybe they weren't feeling as magnanimous about all their tips disappearing as I'd assumed. They concentrated on her face and forearms, the bits that would show, and left her stomach in peace. She got two beautiful black eyes, and some fine bruising on her chin where they'd held her face still for the pummelling. She got her council flat. Just in time, too: Freddy told her she couldn't work any more the week after, as she was turning his club into a freak show. She came back a fortnight after the birth though, and we all fussed over baby while she went on stage and earned a bloody fortune. Feminism in action.

Occasionally we'd get 'Modelling' talent scouts popping in, and soon I got my first modelling shoot, for *Janus* magazine. I played an aerobics instructor, wore a leotard and legwarmers, and took a very gentle spanking from an eager old man in a studio in Camden. It was brilliant fun, and I was really good at it. I found, after all that dancing, I knew exactly how to pose and show myself to best effect. I learnt how spanking photographers manage to time the click exactly to the impact of the hand on flesh, using a metronome, and exactly how to wrinkle up my forehead as though I were in pain. I did another shoot at a council flat in Streatham – toddling off by myself, like an idiot, to meet a man I didn't know, and take my knickers off for him. As usual, I was luckier than I deserved: he was utterly charming and full of good advice as to how I should pursue a career in porn, should I choose to. I didn't choose to – at least, not at that point – but it was interesting stuff nevertheless.

And it was at the Sunset Strip that I met Finlaye. She burst in to the dressing room one morning, all blonde dreadlocks and bosom, bellowed "Alright then, smellies?" and sank down into the most comfortable chair, as though she'd already devoted a decade to the noble art of striptease, although in fact, this was her first audition. She was completely penniless, and had wandered in just on the off chance, having come down from Sheffield to London on the promise of a modelling job that hadn't transpired. The details of the modelling job, she breathlessly informed me over endless cups of sugary tea, were shouted at her from a moving car, just as she was off to the doctors to discuss the possibility of having her gargantuan, comedy, 34FF breasts reduced on the NHS. This mysterious talent scout, who operated from the back of a Ford Fiesta, had mercifully persuaded her otherwise, and so her porn career was born. It's tricky to make a decent living from topless modelling, however, unless you are right at the top of the tree, and so she thought she might give stripping a whirl.

Everything that happened to Finlaye, it seemed, was just a delightful accident. I'd never met anyone so happy-go-lucky. She stayed in a hostel in Kings Cross most nights, except when she managed to pick someone up, when she'd 'Go home with them to save the £20'. She was noisy and outrageous, petite aside from her ludicrous great gazungas, and her seven-inch nails, which were always beautifully decorated – she would spend hours painting them, covering them in glitter or studs, drawing minute snowscapes or sunshine scenes, according to the season. I admired her tremendously. And my God, how she could drink! She made me look like an amateur. She never seemed to eat, but put away pints of lager from first light till the first encounter with her bed for the evening.

Quite often we would do double acts together, since she quickly got bored of spending eight minutes on her own, without anyone to gossip with. She couldn't be bothered with all the sexy wiggling stuff, but went in for comedy strip routines instead, taking a newspaper from a chap on the left, and gravely distributing a sheet to every audience member. Then she'd take the glasses from everyone in the front few rows, jam them onto her knockers and stuff them down her pants, and then do a strange belly dancing routine, which ended with a big pile of spectacles on the stage. There must have been the strangest, most panicked scenes in the auditorium after we'd left: half-blind audience members trying to retrieve their eye-wear whilst obeying the cast iron law that they mustn't talk to, acknowledge, or make eye contact with any other member of the audience.

Eventually she moved in with me. She'd been hinting about it for ages, and had spent a couple of nights dossing on my floor when her lucky pants had let her down. I was living in Hendon, northwest London with the boyfriend I still wasn't quite sure I wanted. I saw very little of him, so I got very little opportunity to really make up my mind. He'd leave for work at 6 a.m., and I'd crawl home at about 1 a.m. and try not to wake him with my drunken stumbling: on Sundays we'd wake together and both look baffled at the stranger by our side. Then he liked to go to Ikea to buy oddly shaped furniture called 'Smurf' and 'Froog', with no clearly defined place or purpose, which in any case he hadn't the ability to assemble. So I was rather pleased to have someone come to stay that I actually liked.

Theoretically, she was meant to pay rent, but in practice she was generally too skint, somehow, despite earning more than most at the Sunset. I didn't care. She was opening my eyes to a whole new way of being, and I loved her for it. Now my Sundays were spent having my nails blinged up, my hair bleached, my pubes and eyebrows ripped away, or shooting zombies on the PlayStation she'd brought home one day after a windfall at work. She continued her modelling, too. One day she had to take a bus to a field somewhere deep in rural Essex, to sit topless on the back of a 'frozen' cow – literally frozen: there were patches of ice on its back – for a Milk Marketing Board calendar. I still have a photo from that shoot somewhere. She's grinning quite convincingly, despite the goosebumps, and the nipples sticking out like thimbles.

That Christmas we worked side by side on the Sunset Christmas show, a tradition in which a collection of large, white, Styrofoam balls were placed on the stage for us to chuck at the audience, who then chucked them back. We wore red dresses and Santa hats, and cavorted to Christmas carols, while all the tips we received were divided fairly among all the participants, right down to the penny. Freddie doubled our drink money during December, so we were all of us pretty much drunk pretty much all of the time. Then the Sunset Strip closed for a week. Steve, the boyfriend, went to Scotland to see his parents; Finlaye went to Sheffield; I went home to Hertfordshire, rich, content, replete. When I came back to London on January 2nd, the Sunset Strip had changed hands, so that Finlaye and I were out of a job, and Steve had filled the flat with even more half-finished hunks of tat from Ikea. Arse and bugger. Bugger and arse.

January is a slack time for the sex trade. Finlaye was better off than me, with her occasional modelling work, but I was well and truly unemployed and seemingly unemployable, at least for a couple of months. I was bored shitless. Fin and I used to go to auditions together occasionally, but they would usually want her and not me, which was dispiriting, particularly when she refused to take the job out of loyalty to me, which meant neither of us could pay the damn rent. Eventually she got a job at the Candy Bar, a lesbian pole-dancing club, which I absolutely insisted that she take since I (as her honorary girlfriend) would be allowed to sit at the bar drinking free of charge all night. She only lasted one night, though. Lesbians are surprisingly gropey, and one dug her nails into Finlaye's left breast until she drew blood. Shame – it was a good gig. Then we had a stint working at a rip-off dive of a hostess bar, with a handful of former dancers from the Sunset Strip.

We had to be there at 8 p.m., even though no one turned up until well after the pubs shut. It was too dark to read and too loud to talk, so we all just sat, glumly, staring at one another. No nudity necessary here: just cocktail frocks, smiles, and a willingness to tolerate and fleece drunken fools. After a couple of hours tedium the management set us to work peeling labels off bottles of cheap Cava, and replacing them with ones that said '1906 Krug', although you'd have to be pretty drunk not to see that they'd been run up on someone's computer.

Eventually two idiots walked in – tourists with very little English, so the headache inducing music levels didn't much matter – and picked Finlaye and India, one of the Spanish sisters, to go sit with them. They ordered two bottles of our newly doctored Cava, and half an hour later they were presented with a bill for £700. India didn't drink, so whenever her glass was filled she made a play of glugging it, then tipped it onto the floor when they weren't looking. It was enough to break my heart. Warm, sour Cava never looked so appetising. I spent the next four hours sculpting a little white reindeer out of the molten candle wax that had dripped on to our table.

Finlaye made £50 that night, Cava commission, but we didn't go back. When we left at 3 a.m. there was a noisy altercation between a bouncer and one of the tourists, who'd sobered up enough to realise he'd effectively been mugged. They were starting to shove each other when we ran off. A few weeks later, we heard a chap had been shot dead there. We didn't need it, we decided. With my fine grasp of English and her knockers we could definitely do better. And yet we didn't, for a couple more months. Finlaye started working at a hairdressers for a bit, to keep us in PlayStation games and pizza. I found occasional work as a market researcher. My God, it was ghastly. All the effort and energy ordinary people had to exert, just to earn a few pounds! I admired them tremendously, really I did, but I wasn't going to keep them company.

Our luck turned when we'd just about given up, and it was my minge that saved us. Nina, the girl who'd helped me through my first audition, rang unexpectedly to say she was newly and gainfully employed finding girls for niche porn. She was traipsing round Eastern Europe trying to find girls who were unusually hairy, at least by western standards, when she remembered my peculiar resistance to shaving.

"Is very good job," she told me, with the energy and zeal of one who worked largely on commission.

"Lots of work, magazine, film, website, all you want. Webcam use you once a week at least. You make good living easy."

It couldn't be worse than market research, anyway. She gave me the number.

"Tell Sean that Nina sent you!"

Finlaye spent her last quid on a celebratory bottle of cider, convinced my muff would be an end to all our woes. With her newly acquired hairdressing skills, she insisted on shampooing and conditioning my groin warmer, bouffing it up with mousse and spray, and talking admiringly about my crop, our harvest, that would see us through the winter. She even started growing her own, but mine had taken years to achieve, and her own thin, wispy, blonde little strands didn't promise anything too spectacular. Instead she concentrated her efforts on my neglected appearance, helping me choose an outfit, doing my makeup and hair, both ends.

Sean had an office in Golders Green, stocked with bright lights and cheap wine. He was a lean, gangly man, deadly professional, completely uninterested in my young self except as a tool to earn him money, which is always reassuring. Girls, you really needn't worry you'll be molested and harassed by porn barons and pimps if you get into the sex trade. All the ones I've ever met are either gay, or sick to death of flange. You're a product to them, nothing else.

"Clara? In here, please darling. Could you drop your pants?"

And I did. In fact, I nearly dropped my pants at the market research interview: I'd never been for a job where it wasn't their first question. Sean ran his fingers through my pelt, as if he were considering buying a rug.

"Mmm-hmm. Not bad. How long have you growing this?" He made it sound like a career choice, rather than laziness and a propensity to shaving rash.

"Um – ten years or so."

"Do you shave anywhere?"

"Just a bit, here, on the inner thigh."

"Well, stop it."

I kissed goodbye to swimming pools and bikinis.

"Fair enough."

"I'm sure I can get you some work. Mainly Yank stuff. They're nuts for it. It's the new taboo. And webcam work. Done webcam before?"

"No."

"It's easy. Can you read?"

I could.

"You'll be fine then. Read what the punters say to you, respond, type something flirty back if you like. Two-hour sessions, £200 a time, ok?"

"God, yes!" He grinned at me then.

"I'll set you up with some photographic work too. You'll be fine. And if you see any other hairy girls, pass 'em my way, won't you?"

He turned back to his computer, where he was photoshopping a little extra bush onto a pair of dusky thighs, and I assumed I had been dismissed.

The next day I got a phone call inviting me to a webcam studio, the location of which was a mysteriously well-kept secret. I was instructed to 'Come alone… and wear something dowdy.' It was in a pretty rural part of England I'd never heard of, an awfully long way to travel when you're skint: Finlaye had to pawn one of her many engagement rings to raise the train fare. Even now, 14 years later, I'm nervous about mentioning the exact location in case I wake up next to a horse's head.

A slight, dark middle-aged man with a limp and a shy smile opened the door to me, in an industrial unit in the middle of nowhere, and quickly ushered me inside.

"Find the place ok? You didn't ask for directions, did you? No one saw you walk up?"

"Jesus. I don't think so…"

"The landlord thinks that we manufacture precision scientific implements. We got run out of Dagenham last year. We simply can't be too careful. In here, in here – "

He showed me through a cluttered corridor and into a tiny room decked ceiling to floor with monitors. On most of them a skinny girl lay on a bed with her legs spread, pubes glistening proudly, clearly well oiled, with a gigantic dildo stuffed up her. Occasionally she would get up from this uncomfortable looking position to glance at the computer screen before her, smile, and change her position, or do something new, tweak her nipples, show her arse crack. It looked simplicity itself.

"That's Anna. Russian girl. Her English isn't up to much, but she can more or less understand what they are typing to her. See?"

He pointed to a screen filled with text. Sure enough, it showed a line of men's names, followed by instructions: Anna, show us your pink, shove that green dildo in harder, I love your pretty pert tits, will you go out with me, where do you live, I dream about you all day long, and on, and on. It was like a collective male psyche, unfiltered, unedited and rather badly spelt.

"Ideally she'd be writing back to them too, but it's just beyond her grasp of English. But we'd like you to type and strip, if you would."

He looked at me for the first time.

"You'd better get changed and get your slap on doll, you're on in five. The loo's through there."

He pointed to a grubby little cupboard.

"I'll give you a big build up. Don't let me down."

Not being quite certain what my job involved, I wasn't sure how I could let him down, but I nodded and promised fervently that I would Do My Best, and tried to look earnest as I said it. Then I nipped into the loo, where Anna had already taken up most of the available space with a frightening collection of uniforms and props. I'd only brought one dress and a pair of heels. I put them on, feeling rather pathetic and uncertain. Anna had even surrounded the basin with a variety of perfumes. Maybe she needed to smell like a tart to get into character. I picked up one and sniffed it, then smashed it back down guiltily as I heard her approach. She stormed in naked, threw a pile of clothes into the corner, and yelled 'Fucking Bastards!!' in my general direction, then began to brush her hair out furiously, as if it had caused her offence. I made what I hoped were suitably sympathetic noises and scuttled away back to the room of computers, hoping to God I passed muster.

The man with the moustache barely glanced at me, so fascinated was he by his own literary effort.

"There you go doll, cop a load of that!" So cop I did:

'A real treat for you today, a beautiful, sexy lap dancer, never seen before on the World Wide Web! Brunette, green eyes, nice neat tits and a bush to die for!! Gentlemen, start your engines!!!'

He looked up at me proudly.

"Good eh?"

"Very. I just hope I can live up to the notice."

"Acch, you'll be fine. Piece of piss. Come on, I'll show you round the studio. Don't worry, the camera's off."

I tiptoed after him. I was feeling horribly nervous. I'm not a natural beauty, far from it. When stripping, I'd developed a knack for letting my personality shine through, interacting with the punters, wearing an expression which I hope conveyed 'Obviously this is ridiculous, that you're sitting down there while I wiggle about up here showing you the bits I was born with, but let's just make the best of it, shall we?' I hated the idea of not being able to see or manipulate my audience, of being judged only on my appearance.

"Here are your dildos, which are sterilised every night."

I categorically did not believe that.

"More batteries, if you need them. Nipple clamps, paddles, all that sort of thing, are over here."

Was I meant to torture myself as well?

"And here's the keyboard. You can see yourself up here on that monitor, and you can see what they're typing here."

They were already typing, wondering among themselves what the new girl would be like, if she'd be as awful as Sally or as fat as Pam. This did nothing to assuage my fears.

"The cameras are here, here and here. When they're on, you have to assume some one can see your every move. No picking your nose, or reading a book. You're on stage for the whole two hours. Got it?"

"Got it. I think. And – but –" as he went to turn on the cameras, panic rose in me " – What exactly do I do?"

"Whatever they tell you to do, of course. Within reason."

He paused to consider.

"And I wouldn't penetrate yourself with the bedpost if I were you. Anna has already done that today, and I'm not sure she's totally clean."

I looked at the bedpost, which was the size of a sturdy bollard, and assured him I wouldn't. He crept out of the room. I sat on the bed and looked at the screens. A terrified looking girl, pale and exhausted, stared back at me. I sat up straight and tried a cheeky wink. Not so bad after all. The light was wonderfully flattering. The other screen, filled with text, started scurrying past my eyes like ticker tape.

- Hello
- Hello new girl
- Are you really new?
- What's your name then?

- Take your knickers off
- Have you got a boyfriend?

A disembodied voice suddenly boomed into the room.

"Darling, I meant to say, get your tits out by 2.30, your bush by 3 and stay naked for the final hour, ok?"

I nodded.

"Don't nod! They can see you, remember? Type something back to 'em!"

I looked down at the worryingly oily keyboard, and wondered what to type first. All those conflicting demands kept coming.

- Show us how wide you can spread your legs
- How many fingers can you get in?
- Do you make a lot of noise when you cum?
- Do you know Destiny she's a lap dancer too?
- Can you give me your number. I'm an amateur photographer, you can trust me.

I took a deep breath and started typing. Typing I could do.

- Hello everyone. My name's Clara. I'm new here, and new to webcam, but I've been in the sex industry for three years and I'm not an idiot.
- Who'd like to explain to me what happens next? The politest answer gets to choose my first pose.

And we were away. They seemed genuinely delighted I could write back to them. Some of them were quite good fun, and we got on famously. The two hours whizzed past. I had to be reminded to take off my clothes and make with the sexy. I picked up a dildo and sniffed at it dubiously. This resulted in a banging on the wall. I tried to pass it off into a sexy licking motion. Actually, it did taste slightly of disinfectant. I was probably safe after all.

The job consisted entirely of lying on a bed and occasionally sitting up to type bollocks, two occupations at which I excelled. I learnt how everyone started going quiet, or making ridiculous typos, the ruder I became – the trials of typing left-handed, presumably. Moustache man seemed pretty pleased with me, muttering about click rates and viewing figures, and promising me a regular slot each week. Perched on top of my bag I found an envelope with 'Hirsute: £200' scribbled on it. Inside were ten limp notes. Salvation.

I did a few hairy porn shoots, stills and film, after that, all ludicrously well paid and – well, just ludicrous. Modelling was dull and physically demanding – they were determined to get their money's worth out of their models, so I would usually spend 12 hours or so in the most extraordinary positions, legs behind my head, doing shoulder stands in the bath, leaning backwards out of windows, legs splayed, all to show off my genitals in new and unusual ways. Luckily I was pretty flexible. I developed an ability to go off into a zen-like trance state, and would come to, to find a young man crouched between my thighs, brow furrowed, camera the size of an elephant's head flashing away at my lady parts. The Americans liked to learn something about the models too, so at the end of each shoot I would be presented with a four-page questionnaire, asking me the most baffling questions. What was my favourite pudding? How old was I when I was first kissed? Who was my most embarrassing celebrity crush? What was my position on capital punishment? God knows what the Russian girls made of it. I answered diligently, but not having ever seen any of these magazines, I've no idea how much they used. Probably a single speech bubble, like the page three girls. 'Clara, 23, stopped pruning her bush 12 years ago, quite fancies Will Self, and thinks universal nuclear disarmament is a goal towards which every nation should strive!'

Finlaye discovered she was pregnant around this time. She hid it as long as she could, with corsets and fanciful stories about trapped wind and beer bellies, but at seven months she was chucked out of her lap dancing job. God knows why: she was earning a bloody fortune. Men love the pregnant girls, as long as they're not married to them. She did a little 'Poppin Mama' porn after that, but found it too perverted even for her taste, and decided to go back home to her parents in Sheffield. I missed her dreadfully. When the baby arrived, its head was quite flat on one side, 'from all the corsets'. A birthmark with a quality anecdote.

I decided to chuck my on-off boyfriend, largely because I wanted a baby too, and he emphatically did not. I had accumulated a decent amount of money, and bought myself a pretty cottage in the suburbs. The neighbours were politely suspicious of my youth and independence. I started a rumour that I had inherited most of my wealth and did a little freelance tuition for the rest, which hurt my pride horribly, given I'd spread my legs for every sodding brick. But you can't go shouting that sort of thing in Hertfordshire. So there I was, 23, with a pretty house, a ridiculously well paid career, and a hankering to become a mother. It seemed the next logical step in my ludicrous existence. What was the point of all this material wealth if I had no one to share it with and bequeath it to? I decided to find a man. Not a partner, I didn't aspire to that, just a jizz donor. I thought it couldn't be too difficult. After all, I met hundreds of the things every day, walking sperm tubes, all generally babbling about their keenness to fill me with baby porridge. I started working the London pub strip circuit, accumulating so much cash it became a fire hazard, but always with my eye out for a suitable chap.

When I started, there were over seventy pubs in London and Essex which offered nude dance along with your pint. Most have closed down now, or put a stop to the nudity. We have entered an incredibly moralistic age. Feminism came to mean being anti-sex, and mysteriously the feminists won: we all have to pretend we hate sex now, and that women earning a good living having a jolly time is somehow disgraceful. A combination of overzealous regulations from Westminster

City Council, the general decline of pubs, topped off with the smoking ban, means it's nearly impossible to earn a living doing the circuit now. In 1999, though, they were at their peak, and the ugliest idiot could have made her fortune within a couple of years.

This is how the pubs worked. An agency had a couple of hundred girls on its books. Most pubs had a lunchtime and an evening shift, usually requiring two or three girls for each shift. So we were all kept busy pretty much all day, every day. The pubs paid the agent. The chaps didn't pay an entrance fee: instead they'd put a fifty pence piece or a pound coin into our glass as we walked round before our dance. It was wonderfully exciting. We'd do a three-minute dance, and earn perhaps £150 for it on a busy night. Then put our clothes back on, pick up our glasses, and troll back round again, over and over. It was silly money, dirty money, smelling of beer and fags, sticky with sweat and aftershave. How my back would ache of a night, lugging it all back home. God knows what the bank made of me, turning up each morning with sacksful of change. Probably that I was one of those super-successful beggars so beloved of the *Daily Mail*. Not so far off the mark, actually. Each morning I'd take the train into London, my cheap, battered old hold-all stuffed full of sequins, boas, crusty old knickers, CDs and sandwiches, and every night come back quite tipsy and weighed down with money. It's a wonder I was never mugged, chinking steadily as I wove my way along. But I suspect the neighbours may have started to suspect I wasn't the quiet heiress and private tutor I claimed to be.

Stripping makes you racist. And ageist, and classist, and all the other ists. Faced with a roomful of chaps, you need to make some instant decisions about where you should best spend your time to maximise your income. Now maybe this was personal to me, but I found the best payers were young white C2s and Ds – the ones who looked like they'd just finished an eight-hour shift on a building site, all covered in plaster and brick dust, and wanted a sit down and a few pints. They had plenty of spare money and that live fast die young approach so beloved of my bank balance. They would invariably greet me with the words, "Cor, you're a bit posh to be doing this, entcha?" so perhaps it was my novelty value that made them cough up. Second to these chaps, suits. The lairy drunken young ones could go either way: pick out the leader, and see if he plans to assert his dominance by spending liberally or prove his manhood by causing you trouble. You'll either make a fortune or waste your time and be soundly insulted. Quiet solo suits will generally provide a steady income, but bore you with their work and marital trouble. Asians will pay, but you have to work for it. They want to know exactly what they will get for their money. Black men don't pay strippers. Must be a cultural thing. They'll hover, but they won't pay. Of course, broad sweeping generalisations, but that's what stripping does to you. If you make the wrong judgement call it could mean the difference between a wretched, humiliating evening and a mortgage payment.

I tried, periodically, to get pregnant, but the men I met were generally such louts I could only bear to spend a single evening of their company. I was living such an unhealthy lifestyle it was probably very lucky that I didn't succeed. I didn't try to deceive men. I'd see a relatively handsome one, shove my pint glass under his nose and say: "Would you like to contribute to my dance, please?" and once he'd obliged, "And would you like to make me pregnant too?" I'd explain I required no financial or emotional support, just a few drops of that stuff I seemed to elicit so naturally anyway.

The agency was arranged alphabetically, so I generally found myself working with Chrissie, Christina, Claire, Clarissa and Courtney, without any idea what Annabel or Zenka, about whom I'd heard so much (none of it complimentary) might be like. Of my co-initialled colleagues, I liked Chrissie best. She was posh, plump and absurdly overqualified, writing a PhD on Medieval Popes, of all things, and forever suffering marital trouble, of which I heard more than I would have chosen.

There were a lot of quiet afternoons spent sitting in bars in Shoreditch, buying each other pint after pint, and discovering her partner's peculiarities. Josh was the jealous type. Why would a jealous type marry a stripper? Beats me. Maybe he liked the drama. Every half hour she had to ring him to explain how bored she was, how utterly un-turned-on. It was nearly impossible to get into a rhythm with any punters with that nonsense carrying on.

"He found a stain on my skirt," she confided in me, as we sat gobbling chips one rainy Monday lunchtime, waiting in vain for the bankers to stop banking and pop in for a perv and a pint. "He was absolutely convinced it was spunk. But it was mayonnaise! He thinks I'm having an affair with a bloody jar of Hellmann's!"

I tutted sympathetically and tried to avoid looking at my watch. Slow days were a killer. I was sure I could feel my face wrinkling, my ovaries withering. Chrissie hid her chips under her frock as the landlord walked past.

"I'm giving this lark up," she went on, poking suspiciously at a pube on her chip box. I'd heard that before, almost daily, and told her so.

"No, really. I mean it. I'm getting a job where he just can't be suspicious of me, somewhere –"

A crèche? A nunnery?

"Somewhere where the money is so quick I just wouldn't have time to do anything else. He just won't believe that I can spend ten hours in the pub, and come home with £30…"

Had he not seen her drink?

"I'm thinking about strippergrams. Fancy it?"

"Um…"

"My mate Michelle runs this agency, and they're always looking for girls. The joy of the strippergram is, whatever the hell it is you're walking in to, you know it'll all be over in five minutes. And they've booked you, they want you, and you know you're gonna make someone's night. Beats sitting around here all day, waiting for someone to notice you, no?"

"Hmmm… I dunno…"

"There'd be no talking to 'em, no hanging about. You get four or five a night, and that's an easy £200, and the whole day to yourself too."

It did sound extraordinarily attractive. I could spend all my days meditating, drinking smoothies and painting the nursery, rather than hanging out in bloody smoky bars. Chrissie pushed a business card at me.

"Go on, give her a call."

I did, the next day. The decision was rather made for me when a banker finally showed up at the bar, picked me to do lap dance after lap dance in the roped off area in the corner, demanded to see my bottom at closer and closer quarters, my bottom cheeks spread as wide as I could make 'em, pressed almost onto his nose – until finally the inevitable happened, and I farted in his face. He was appalled, and shouted about it rather noisily. As if his particular predilections were my fault.

I spoke to Michelle, an elderly sounding woman with a thick Essex accent. I gave her my by now immense CV of relevant experience, she sounded suitable impressed, and explained the job to me. It sounded easy enough and indeed, wonderfully quick. I promised to start looking into obtaining some policewoman and traffic warden uniforms, and to call her when I was ready to begin. Ten minutes later she rang me back.

"Actually, could you do one this lunchtime?"

"Oh God, really?"

"Yeah, it's meant to be me, but I really can't be bothered."

She stripped… this woman who sounded like my Granny?

"It's a 40th birthday, at the Harvester in Harrow."

A Harvester, on a Sunday lunch time? Was that even allowed? Surely it would be swarming with kids?

"Ach, it's only a topless. You're meant to be a policewoman, claiming he's parked illegally, but you can just say you're plain-clothed!"

She cackled heartily at this. Turned out it was one of her favourite jokes.

"The victim's name is Steve. The contact is Dave. He'll meet you outside the pub at 1.30, with cash, £60, of which I get £20. Got it?"

I got it. A baptism of fire. This seems, I now realise, to be the theme of all these stupid jobs. They want you now, yesterday for preference. Small wonder I struggled with the rigmarole of real work, CVs, interviews, references, DBS checks: in my world you decide you're low on cash, and five minutes later you've got some. 'In and out in five minutes', I kept telling myself on the drive. I knew that pub. I had eaten there with my mum. It seemed just extraordinary to be marching in there now and getting my knockers out. Just imagine it, ambling into one of your favourite pubs and stuffing some secondary sex organs into the face of a stranger, probably while he was eating his roast and his kids were running round his ankles, hyped up on Cola. Imagine that. You'd probably refuse, wouldn't you? Shake your head in wonder that anyone could ask something so ludicrous of you? So why the hell didn't I?

I cobbled together a rubbish police outfit, consisting of short, tight black skirt, white blouse, hold-ups and high heels, and a silky black scarf knotted vaguely round my neck. It didn't matter a bit though, as they were all expecting me, and insisted rather noisily that I remove my clothes as soon as I walked in. I closed my eyes, and did as I was told. Heaven knows what time they'd all started drinking, but most of them could barely stand. I had to chase my victim round the dinner table, in true Benny Hill style, and eventually half sit on him while I removed my clothes. Handcuffs, I thought: next time I'll bring handcuffs. And a truncheon. The boys all called for the victim to be given a birthday spanking, which I gladly gave. They also seemed to think that my tits should be covered in whipped cream and wobbled in his face. I explained that I'd only been in the job less than an hour, and hadn't had time to pick any up. A leftover bowl of ice cream was procured from a nearby table, and substituted, to reasonable effect. It was a bloody sticky business, though. I popped into the ladies for a quick wash down, but the scowls and glares I received there soon sent me scuttling away again. Another note to self: next time, bring wet wipes.

Girls, know this: taking your clothes off in front of men makes them happy and mellow, but repeat the trick in front of girls and the girls get very cross indeed. Also: men aren't the least bit fussy. With very few, probably gay, exceptions, men don't notice saggy tits, pot bellies or a touch of cellulite. They're just so pleased that you're naked, the rest is a blur. Girls, however, won't rest easy until you've been pulled to pieces. Over the delicious sound of chaps panting, I could still make out a low undercurrent of female mutter: look at the size of her arse! I could do better than that! And why the hell doesn't she trim that minge?

Such dreadful insecurity among women is, of course, a tragedy and a blight, and I would really like to have told all these girls the secret: men really don't care how you look, so it's pointless being jealous of me. But if I'd got any closer, they'd probably have glassed me.

Michelle must have got a good report back, because I got the job. Strippergrams tended to happen back-to-back on a Friday and Saturday night, so I had the rest of the week for myself for webcam and porn, and the odd well paid pub shift. The most money, by far, though, was from those weekend strippergrams. I very much enjoyed the work, aside from all the endless driving and getting lost. I got to know Herts, Essex and North and East London so well I could probably have turned cabbie, if I'd fancied. I found myself a police helmet and a naughty nurse's outfit, and was rarely asked for anything else. The nurse thing was quite often requested at residential homes, to celebrate patients ninetieth or hundredth birthdays – always nerve-wracking grinding away on a centurion's lap, fearing you might be the death of them, or start your shift coated in bodily fluids. Occasionally I was asked to turn up as a nun, and I would improvise with a black sheet and a crucifix; once I was asked to dress as a 'grungy art student' for the opening night of some surreal play – I turned up at the after-show party and manage to snaffle a fair few canapés before I found the director, and took off my luminous tutu and stripy leotard, to thunderous applause.

The worse type of gig was generally in an office. Horrid fluorescent lighting, no atmosphere, Tuesday 11 a.m. and me trying to get through security to see Mark in accounts, who was 50 yesterday, and is today nursing a banging hangover. Most of my gigs were in pubs, with music, booze and chatter as a backdrop, and I hardly ever remembered to bring a stereo with me. The three minutes I spent disrobing to total, stunned silence, 22 office workers staring at me joylessly, the women scowling, the men shocked and nervous at their own arousal, must have been the longest of my life. Even if I remembered a CD player, in those huge, echoey offices its tinny, trilling pop beats seemed to make the whole experience even more pathetic. Still, at least I tried.

I was sent to do a job at a warehouse in Herts, which stocked huge quantities of designer creams and makeup, and came away laden with free samples – what a coup! And I had to do a few in the open air, on building sites, with special protective boots, helmet and fluorescent jacket, and nothing beneath – they were always a giggle. No girls present, and lots of exciting pieces of equipment for me to improvise on.

My stash of coins began to be enhanced and buffeted by bundles of notes. I kept my cash in a Quality Street tin, and took real, nerdy pleasure in watching it grow, week by week. Strippergrams were useless for finding baby-fathers though. If their chief advantage was their speed, it was also their disadvantage. I must have done thousands of the things, shown my gash to tens of thousands of people, but now there are very few I can remember, and those mostly because they were unpleasant. But I enjoyed the job, in the main: it was fun making people's evenings enjoyable, particularly the stag parties, who always looked bored shitless when I turned up, as if they knew they ought to be doing something decadent and crazy, but just couldn't think of anything. I knew just how to handle them. Blindfold, handcuffs, paddle, whipped cream, ice cubes. Lovely.

For a few happy months, I spent my evenings going round a succession of 18th birthday parties in Harrow. Clearly my reputation had spread, and any boy, seeing what his friend had enjoyed on his birthday, would start saving his pocket money months in advance so he could enjoy the same. I'm afraid I teased them dreadfully: nice, well brought up boys all of them, sitting round in a circle enjoying my charms, most of them with cushions on their laps. I revelled in my power, and went as far as I dared with them – might, indeed, have gone a lot further had I not had other appointments waiting, past those boys' bedtimes.

The appointments I most dreaded were those Michelle referred to as 'revenge gigs', where I was roped in to humiliate some poor chap who had doubtless played some practical joke the month before. Usually these gigs went to the Roley-Poley girl, (or 'Grot-a-gram', as she was charmingly advertised): it takes more balls than I'll ever have to sell views of your naked self as a form of punishment, to take your clothes off and expect to elicit laughter. She was a good-natured, single mother in her 40s, and took good care to laugh along with the rest, loudest of all: but she hated the job and spoke very bitterly of the men who paid her. Small wonder. She gave up in the end when an unusually large, vicious and determined stag party actually managed to turn her car upside down while she was getting naked, so when she came out she found it spinning plaintively, on its roof, wheels in the air. Poor girl, with her kids waiting at home for her, and no way to get back to them! She screamed, and cried, and made such a noisy fuss that she amassed a small crowd, who managed to right the car and get her home. But the car was never again the same, and neither was she. She got a job in Asda soon after.

Once, I was called to a 17th birthday at a slaughterhouse. Now I'm the most squeamish of vegetarians, and I desperately didn't want to do it, but the money was terrific, and Michelle insisted. I got through security, and was dressed as a health and safety inspector: hair back in a blue net, long white coat, thick green wellies. Everything in me was screaming that I should run away. I could smell blood and death in the air, and resolved to make the gig as quick as humanly possible.

Thank God, I was led into a small, but decent office – the wellies had made me worried that I might be cavorting in a puddle of entrails. My relief was short-lived, however, as I saw a young boy being pulled towards me by half a dozen lairy, yelling types, all of them covered in blood. It got worse. As the boy got closer, I saw that he had Down's Syndrome. He wasn't entering into the joke at all. He looked terrified and tearful.

I considered jumping out of the window, but it was too sodding high, and I'm no hero. His mates had us both surrounded, and were snarling at me to get on with it. I made the boy sit down, and gave him the tenderest lap dance I could, keeping eye contact, trying to calm him down. I ignored my usual bag of tricks, and just squirmed as erotically as I could, whilst doing my best to ignore the pool of blood and guts on his lap. I took off my white coat, and remembered I was wearing my favourite white lace underwear. Arse. I decided to take off his white coat too. He didn't seem to mind. In fact, he seemed impervious to everything, even his mates' cat calls and taunts, in the face of my pretty, bouncing tits. We had quite a nice time together, and ignored the sadists baying around us. He wanted to shake my hand at the end, but I kissed his cheek instead, working on the assumption he probably hadn't used his cheek to murder any animals. A subdued supervisor handed me the cash and took me back through security. He hadn't had the morning's entertainment, chaos and screaming, he had clearly expected. You'd have thought he'd get enough of that in his daily work, without needing to pay for extra.

At the other extreme, I was asked to a scarily posh part of Hertfordshire to do a full nude strip at a private house – well, 'mansion' would probably be a more appropriate word – at a luncheon party, on Easter Sunday. I wish I could give you an explanation of this, but I have none. I can only guess that one of the guests was making some sort of political statement, or perhaps I was part of a sociological experiment. Nude, remember. Half a dozen couples sat round a huge oak table, laden with port and petits fours, the sun streaming in through the window, *Songs of Praise* howling out of the telly, and me skipping about showing them all my arse. The women tutted, the men turned puce. And when I'd finished the hostess pressed £70 into my hand and said, with a frosty smile, 'That was quite disgusting.' Well, duh! And you paid for it, you dozy mare.

Occasionally I doubled up with the Grot-a-gram or a male stripper, for anniversary parties and the like (and *what* an education that was! The girls would pull and scratch at him until he feared for his sanity: Girls are a perfect nuisance – no sense of propriety), but mainly I worked alone. It made for an odd existence, driving through the night, hundreds of miles, finding lay-bys where I could exchange my schoolgirl outfit for a blonde wig and latex catsuit, then stumbling into oases of bright drunkenness, putting on my happy face for five minutes, before staggering away to do it all over again. I'd arrive home exhausted, sweaty, stinking of sour whipped cream – the bloody stench would get everywhere, and the police hat I kept as a souvenir still stinks of it – and resolve never to do it again. But my purse would bulge thickly with notes, and I found I hadn't the willpower to say no to Michelle's treacly "Now, Clara, I've got a nice local one for you, a 63 year old gentleman's stag do, nice quiet country pub..." and having accepted one, felt it incumbent on me to take some of the grottier bookings too.

Often I would end up taking my mum with me, for company and help with map-reading. Quite often she'd get herself invited into the pub or house, start drinking, and I'd never get her out again. When I had a boyfriend, I'd invite him along instead, finding most men enjoyed feeling protective and proprietorial about their women, barking "No touching!" if a punter got too close. Usually they enjoyed plotting out the routes too, leaving me free to worry about outfits, makeup and the finer details of the scenarios. ("Silver Peugeot 307, parked illegally!" I'd be muttering, as I ran into the pub; or "Anne says you're still a naughty boy, and this one's from her…") It seemed I'd never get chance to give the life up, Michelle being in her 50s, and still insanely popular. But then, quite suddenly, I found myself craving satsumas dunked in marmite. That tore it.

I had always been completely confident that no man would ever want to raise a family with me. (The all-powerful narrator must here break this fictional dream to corroborate the truth of this belief, and commend my younger self for her immense good sense.) In my experience men do not want children. They get bullied or tricked into having children, then leave said children, causing a lot of bother as they go. In so far as they do want children, they don't want them with slags. No, I was on my own. That was fine. I was accustomed to taking what I wanted from the universe, and rather pitied those who expected their futures gift-wrapped and hand-delivered. I asked my handsome gay friend Anthony to knock me up one drunken night, and he agreed that sounded a lark, as long as I didn't expect any money for the little bleeder. I promised I didn't. We had some vague idea we needed a turkey baster, but they're a bugger to purchase in January, so substituted a cake icer from Poundland. Much giggling and mess, a torturous shoulder stand, lo, we created life: to think people say it's precious. Anthony was angry, clever, sarcastic, spiteful, all qualities I prized. I decided to name her Elizabeth, after Gaskell, who made a heap of sensible remarks about single mothers. I loved her the moment I saw the two blue lines appear. More than I'd ever loved anyone, more even than money, than attention. Motherhood was easy. All the other stuff remained problematic.

Now my body was no longer my own, but inhabited by a huge, squirming monster. I stripped until I was 14 weeks gone, took every job going, until my Quality Street tin was bulging with readies. But when the punters' first question was no longer, "How much for a fuck?", but "When are you due?" I thought it was probably time to change course.

I tried to get a proper job for a bit. For now was clearly the perfect time to change career path, four months pregnant, six years of solid sex industry experience behind me: I was an appealing prospect to any employer. I did actually find work, cleaning a huge industrial estate overnight, 8 p.m. till 5 a.m. It was grim, heavy, lonely work. And then – I don't quite remember how it happened: was it an advertisement from the back of a magazine? – I thought I might try my luck working on a sex-line. The pay wasn't much better, but at least I'd be at home watching my belly swell, rather than lugging it and me and a mop round acres of factory floor night after night. And I could work until I went into labour. Hell – probably while I was in labour.

"Aren't you worried its first words will be 'soapy tit wank'?" Finlaye enquired when I told her, always one to get straight to the heart of an issue. I thought I would stop long before baby started talking, preferably a few weeks after birth. I expected to be slipping back into my police outfit and whizzing round the South East's finest hostelries. I was very careful not to put on too much weight. Luckily, my cravings for satsumas and marmite stayed with me throughout, without turning into a career-wrecking passion for cheese or lard.

Luckily, too, I didn't suffer much from morning sickness. Many of the requests on 'Cheap Chat', as it was called, were pretty grim. Men wanted to hear me weeing and pooing. A lot. No trouble, I fixed up a jug of water, a tin of beans and a bowl, which did quite nicely. I got myself quite a sound department set up, in fact. The 'great long zip on my leather boots' was actually the fastening of my sleeping bag. The sound of me rubbing my juicy pussy was actually me flapping the inside of my cheek. I would spank a cushion, rather than myself.

The rare morning when I did feel queasy I would always get the Class A nutters. The man with the mania for public hangings ("Your cock swells and you ejaculate just before you die. You'd like to see that, wouldn't you?"). The chap who liked to wank with sandpaper, with a skewer down his Jap's eye, his sister's knickers in his mouth. And the chicken. Ah, the chicken. He was one of my first, and soon became a regular. He liked to act out a scenario where I caught him, strangled him, plucked him, basted him and put him in the oven, then went "Mmmm, mmmm, mmmm!" as I ate him. He was very sweet. "Bet you're a vegetarian really, aren't you?" he said once, after I'd smothered him in lemon butter and devoured his thighs and wings. I assured him I wasn't, even as I gagged.

Oh, it was dull! Dull, dull, dull. To make ends meet, I sat by the phone for 13 hours a day, and most days I took more than 200 calls, most of them 'one minute wankers', who said very little, and stayed on the line just long enough to get the job done, slamming the phone down at the exact point of orgasm, without even lingering to say they still loved and respected me. I got so good at talking them to orgasm, I quickly found I could do it while still reading my book, and would quite resent anyone who broke my concentration to demand something out of the ordinary. My One Minute Script ran something like this:

"Hi, how are you? I'm *horny*. I'm just lying here all alone, nearly naked and juicy wet. I'm dreaming of taking that big thick cock of yours in my mouth – tasting you, teasing you with my tongue – running it up and down the length of your shaft, gently sucking on your balls, one after the other; then lowering my tight, throbbing wet pussy on to you, riding you, feeling you thrust inside me, over and over, and then crying out in ecstasy as you shoot your *delicious* hot cum…"

That was generally all it took. Over and over I said that. I rigged up a number of phone extensions, so I could make tea, do the ironing, scrub the skirting boards, all while I talked gibberish. It was much trickier when I got a punter who wanted something new and different. My brain ached when I tried to use it, like a limb that's cramped from lack of use. Given my accent, I seemed to get a lot of men who wanted to be dominated. I had bugger all idea what to do with them. I'd get them to spank themselves, or lick the bottom of a handy shoe, but this didn't seem to work very often, and they didn't come back.

A few men wanted me to pretend to be a man, which puzzled me, as gay chat lines are always so much cheaper. But most of them would end the call by saying they were definitely not gay, despite wanting to call me Fred and imagining my huge cock grazing their tonsils. The human capacity for self-deception remains a wonder to me. I learnt an awful lot about some extraordinary and rare fetishes during those five months. Just when I thought I couldn't be shocked any more, some new pervert would call and completely confound me. Like Denny, who liked to be called a 'filthy nigger' and a 'dirty black bastard' while he masturbated. "But I'm a *Guardian* reader!" I kept wailing every minute or so, which only made him wank the harder. There was a funeral director who liked to describe his penchant for corpse-fondling, the necessity of penetrating a corpse before rigor mortis set in, to avoid the orifices 'snapping shut' and trapping the eager member in a rigid and permanent embrace. Sometimes I'd be asked to do a little girl's voice, or listen to how cute the neighbour's six-year daughter was, or call the punter "Daddy"… I'd hang up on those. There was no way of reporting them, and there were a fair few of them about, though not nearly as many as wanted to hear me have a poo, which I suppose should reassure society somewhat.

At almost nine months pregnant, my phone broke mid-shift, and I was fined for missing more than five calls in one day. Vainly did I protest that it wasn't my fault, that the ringer had broken from overuse, and was it any wonder? Actually, I didn't protest very hard. I was fed up with the whole business. My throat hurt from all the fake screams. I never wanted to hear another male voice again. Happily I was due a daughter.

I spent the last week of my pregnancy sitting my finals, and not saying anything to anyone. It was bliss. I resolved to never, ever get on the phone again to anyone, if I could possibly help it, a resolution I have largely kept.

Elizabeth arrived furious, fists clenched, a mass of blonde curls and long limbs. I loved her, loved her. My mum held my hand as I screamed her free. She'll break a few hearts, everyone said. I'd prefer she break bank balances, I'd say, and they'd laugh, but I meant it.

When she was two weeks old, like an idiot, a desperate, greedy idiot, I rang Michelle and claimed my body had snapped back into shape, like magic. It was completely untrue. My belly sagged, I still had my stiches in, and one tit was at least three sizes bigger than the other one. Could I possibly have my old job back? She murmured something noncommittal, and I assumed I'd been replaced. It was sickening. There aren't many jobs a single mum with a new-born can manage, but tearing into a pub, and ripping her clothes off is surely one of them. Arse. My little stash of cash wouldn't last forever. What could I possibly do now?

Twenty minutes later she rang back.

"Could you do a job this afternoon, do you think?

Oh joy! Again, it seemed, I was wanted yesterday. But then again, 'For Christ's sake!' None of my old clothes fitted me. I had been very careful not to put on excess weight, but still, Beth had been a huge baby, 10lb 6oz, and the space where she'd been hiding was surely gonna sag for a bit. I improvised an outfit and shot off to the pub, leaving Beth behind the bar while I did my turn. It was an 18th birthday party. The victim, overexcited and unaccustomed to drink, decided to slip a finger in me once I'd taken my knickers off – me, still with my stitches in! I brought a fist down very sharply on the top of his head; collected my cash and, after a moment's thought, my baby, in dignified silence.

People were always telling me your life changes forever when you have a baby, but I can honestly say that mine didn't, not one bit. I was lucky, no doubt, that Beth was an easy, amenable child, clever and obliging, patient as a cat. She'd go to sleep as soon as we got in the car, most of the time, and usually I'd get my mum to come with us and sit beside her while I did my thing. Back home, I washed the shaving foam off my tits and fed her, on demand, which soon brought my tummy more or less under control. She slept in my bed at night, and I carried her with me everywhere during the day. At the nicer, family parties, I'd take her inside while I slipped off my outfits, and the women would make a fuss of her while the men ogled the body that made her. So the world turns. At one house, a woman gave me £20 'for the pretty one's money box', and begged to be allowed to touch her, 'for luck' – seemed she'd being trying to have kids of her own for years. I hope it helped.

On one occasion, Michelle asked me to include Beth in my routine. I'm not proud of agreeing to her suggestion, although remembering it still makes me smile. It was the birthday of a ghastly, tight-arsed bigot, who apparently was often to be heard complaining of "Bloody immigrants, coming over here, taking our benefits, teaching their kids to beg and steal..." and all that stuff. His chums had come up with the brilliant idea of requesting a stripper with a baby, who would pose as a Kosovan refugee, and go pestering him for money; then, when he loudly and rudely refused, shame him with an incredibly rude, hopefully painful routine. I negotiated a rate for Beth too of course – no BOGOF deals here – and set about planning. Beth was very blonde to be a Kosovan, so I smeared her in dirt and put a dark hat on her to disguise the worst of her Aryan roots. I put her in a hippy papoose thing I'd borrowed, and wore my shabbiest clothes and boots, topped off with a dark shawl and a few smears of dirt for myself. We did look a disreputable pair! In fact, we got a whole carriage to ourselves on the tube. If you suffer from claustrophobia, I wholeheartedly recommend dressing as an asylum seeker.

The gig went perfectly to plan. It was in quite a posh restaurant, but the manager had been warned to expect me. The only problem was where to put Beth once I'd revealed my identity and needed to remove my mucky clothes. One of the bigot's friends looked quite cuddly and paternal, I thought, so I handed the child over while I spanked and bullied the birthday boy. Beth started to whimper hungrily once she saw my tits pop out, and hearing her made me spurt milk all over the bigot's face, which delighted his friends. I was asked to stay for dinner, and we all had a wonderful time in each other's company, even the bigot, and especially Beth, who was much admired and got all the tit she could handle.

Soon after this I got a follower, who was only too happy to read the maps and babysit while I made the money – we'd first met on the wank-line, and over the course of several evenings we'd devised a code whereby he could find out my phone number. He'd stay every weekend and help. He proved so useful I married him, in time, after several hundred strippergrams. I drove us to Prague for the wedding. He read the map. Beth carried the rings.

Chapter Twelve

"Wait. So this is your – current husband? The one you just want back to?"

"No. Another one. Alex. He cleared off after a decade or so."

I'd been blogging next to my do-gooder, whose name, it had transpired, over many days of companionable keyboard tapping, was Richard. I'd cranked out a good 30,000 words by now. I'm very competitive. And home was still weird. We typed and typed. It helps to keep posting links to this shit on Twitter. Keeps their minds freshly full of you. And honestly, I was enjoying remembering this stuff. A lifetime of leg-spreading. Apparently he'd stopped pretending he was much too busy with his own work to read mine.

"Why did he go?"

I shrugged. "Oh, I dunno. That's what men do, isn't it? He met someone else. We're still in touch. He's turned into a right wanker, which is some consolation. Here –"

I logged on to Facebook to show him Alex, handsome and chiselled, standing among a crowd of raggedy sorts, holding spades aloft and cheering.

"He's co-chair of the refugee allotment project now. Alongside his new wife. Karen."

"Do they allot refugees or make them weed raspberries?"

"The latter. Urban, educated refugees in the main, who are desperate to have their medical or legal qualifications recognised, but they get them handling manure and digging potatoes because they've decided that's best for their mental health. It also makes for some lovely social media posts, although doubtless that's coincidental. They supply food banks, a virtuous circle, Eritreans feeding Britain's impoverished children. Isn't that lovely?"

"Lovely."

I scrolled and tutted.

"I see he's begging for the tender-hearted to sponsor his hike through Norway to raise money for a new shed. I suppose it would be churlish to point out he could buy twenty sheds for the cost of a flight to Norway, and that he's always rather liked walking, and herring. Still, you don't get many likes for just shutting the fuck up and nipping down B&Q, do you? Where's the fun in that?"

"None."

"Nor indeed for being kind or loyal to your wife or stepdaughter. He was an angry, opinionated, controlling brute. I don't want to remember it. It was a mistake, that's all. I was glad he went, except he took everything. House, car, savings. Left me only my legs and accent. Happily that's all I need. You married?"

He shifted in his chair. "Divorced. Ten years now."

"You don't like being asked questions, do you? Or talking about yourself. Is that why you're a journalist?"

"Have you ever thought about getting this stuff published?"

"Oh that's it, evade the question, don't even bother to hide it. Nah. Eee, you could write a book, people always say, when they can't think of anything else to say. But no one would publish me. I don't know the right people or the right words to make that kind of thing happen. I'll stick to my blog, cheers. Why did you get divorced?"

"I was a shit."

"Ah." I rummaged for my purse. "Accept the things you cannot change. I'll drink to that. You up for another?"

"Of course."

"You got kids?"

"Two."

"Are you seeing anyone now?"

"No." And he returned pointedly to his laptop. Fine. Except –

"Well, why not? You're handsome and you've got a proper job and all that. You're a good listener. Don't girls like that sort of thing anymore?"

"They do. But I'm picky. I don't fall in love easily and it takes so much time and energy to hang out with people waiting for love to happen. I can't be bothered."

"I see."

"That's not a come on, by the way."

"No, I realise that."

"I mean it really isn't. It sounded like one, I know –"

"I got it! Jeez, my life is complicated enough, thanks."

He was typing busily when I'd got back. Barely acknowledged his fresh beer. Where had I got to? The marriage, yeah. Look, I don't have to write about the things I don't want to write about, do I. It happened, that's all. Bloody boring bastard remembering. It happened, move on. I wanted a posh boy to want me and he did, briefly, then got embarrassed at his youthful foibles and cleared off to save the world. Very publicly. I carried on. You don't need one man when you're adored by hundreds.

Chapter Thirteen

I continued to strip, but the gigs seemed to be getting rougher. The Grot-a-gram girl got the worst of this, being mouthy and feisty and usually spoiling for a fight. On one job, a girl followed her into the loo and punched her in the face, splitting her lip with a huge sovereign ring. God knows why – she can't have felt jealous or threatened by her. Her entire act consisted of her humiliating herself and sending herself up. Perhaps this girl thought she was so vile and repulsive she needed punishing, or something. Anyway, she drove herself to hospital, one hand on the steering wheel, the other trying to hold together the two pieces of her lip and stem the flow of blood. Ah, why bother trying to understand how these peoples' minds work?

It was frightening to hear about. But nothing like that ever happened to me. I had a few unpleasant altercations, but nothing I couldn't handle. I'd perfected a posh, charming, dopey persona, all smiles and amiability, so people seemed to feel more inclined to laugh at me than want to hurt me. Suited me. But I did go to a gig that stopped me, all the same. It was in deepest Essex – not far from the webcam place – a young lad's stag-do. The contact met me at the door with the cash.

"Where's your minder, then?"

I got that a lot.

"I don't have one. No need."

"No, you'll be fine. Don't worry."

"I'm not," I said, indifferently, and we walked in. There were about thirty of them, and they encircled me in a tight rugby scrum. They ripped my clothes from me, and took them, and my bag, with car keys, money and phone in, and I was assaulted by seemingly hundreds of fists and fingers. It was extraordinary behaviour. I'd never encountered anything like it. Eventually one of them staggered back, and I fought my way out of the circle, but without clothes or bag I couldn't think what to do next. They were blocking the front door, anyway. I ran out into the pub garden, naked. It was surrounded by a high brick wall with no obvious way out or in, so I tried to climb it, but I fell back, grazing a few bits. A man came over to me, helped me up and put his jacket around me. I didn't know if he was one of the stag party, or a barman, or just another customer: I wasn't taking much in. But he walked me back through the pub, fending off and punching a few of the stag party as they tried to get another grope in. He lent me his phone so I could call the AA and get back into my car, and Michelle, so I could cancel the rest of my work – a piss poor strippergram I would have made, turning up already naked.

Michelle called the police, despite my protestations. They turned up, along with an ambulance, which seemed completely over the top. I showed them the few pathetic marks on my arms and legs, and they tutted, but clearly there wasn't much to see. They recommended I get checked out for STDs, although I doubt there's much you can contract from fingers, however mucky. The police went into the pub and managed to retrieve my bag, although by now it was empty, and a battered policewoman's hat. I tossed it onto the back seat, wrapped myself in the foil blanket the ambulance man had left, and drove home.

I was astonished by what had happened to me, and furious too. Later, though, I was scared to death. I couldn't stop revisiting that evening over and over in my head, wondering how I could have handled it better, how I could have acted differently for a happier outcome. But it seemed that whoever had walked into that situation would have met a similar fate. They were spoiling for a fight, that was all. It was nothing personal. Any more than me grinding my snatch against someone's face was anything personal, or covering them in shaving foam and beating them senseless. We were all just doing what we had to do.

But even while I knew that, I also knew I didn't want to do it anymore. I'd been in the sex industry for ten years at this point. Ten years! I didn't have a clue how to do anything else. I had a degree, but much good that would do me with a blank CV and no skills to boast about. I slumped into hopelessness. And I had to go on working, had to. I would get terribly drunk to do it, so I asked my mum to drive me round, and went into the gigs like an automaton, starting at the least noise or sudden movement. It was no fun for anyone. I started applying for random jobs, lying brazenly on application forms. I still didn't get anywhere. I tried to work at the post office, a care home, a refuge for the victims of domestic abuse. Nothing. Eventually I was offered a job working at a call centre. They didn't care about my history: they were only interested in my charming, dulcet tones, so distinct from the flat estuary English that characterised my neighbours' speech, so useful for flogging insurance. It was a crap job, long hours, tiny salary. I started to realise how extraordinarily lucky I'd been having a job that involved me leaving the house just an evening a week, that still paid all the bills. I missed Beth terribly, and I was skint. No, this was no way to live! Like a normal person? I think not. All well and good for the people who are born to it, but for me? Never.

I knew, of course, that strippers had a limited shelf life, anyway. I didn't want to become a joke, lugging my tired old tits out of my basque decade after decade. I'd heard the sneers when some of the older girls danced – "Brought your Grannie along for a day out, have you? Isn't that nice?" – girls who, I now realised, were barely older than me. I wasn't prepared to become a comedy turn, not just yet. What did girls do, in those long, long years between being barely legal and Grot-a-grans?

I scoured the internet for answers. One line of enquiry particularly attracted me, and recurred in my research more than most. It would suit all of my talents – my fabulous legs, my clipped accent, my imagination, my adventurous nature – and suit my personality too. It was so obvious I couldn't believe it hadn't occurred to me before. I would become a Dominatrix.

A website group down in the South West of England was advertising for models. They had half a dozen websites, largely female to male spanking, a few female-to-female. I signed up for a day's work, involving a handful of films, some where I'd be receiving, most where I'd be dishing it out. I thought it would make an excellent introduction to my new career. And it meant £200, which by this time I badly bloody needed. I'd spoken to Tara on the phone and she sounded charming.

"Bring all your clothes" she told me. "All of them. We'll have a rummage through and see what's suitable."

The director didn't like to plan ahead, apparently: he received inspiration from the outfits the girls chose to bring, believing this would express their inner personalities.

"He sounds a prick!" I told her gaily, although as soon as I'd said it I knew she was going to tell me the prick was her boyfriend. She did. She was very nice about it. And when I turned up, he was actually quite charming. I packed my battered policewoman's outfit, a slutty schoolgirl costume, a few glittery stripper dresses, a leather basque, and a couple of smart suits. All he wanted, however, was the manky top and jeans I'd travelled down in, sweating nervously every second.

We did have fun! It was a pretty small, budget operation, with his mate, Gary, doing the camera work, David directing. We spent the first hour taking photos of me being spanked – not hard, just enough to show the impact on my flesh. They kept up a nice steady rhythm so the photographer would know exactly when to take the picture. It was very restful. Then I spanked Tara, although as a pro-sub she had a hide like rhino, and I could barely make a dent on her. When she spanked me, however, the cameraman politely told me that my screaming was making a mockery of his sound levels. There is a knack to taking a spanking. You have to think of the heat as something pleasant, like a tropical sun beating down on your glistening buttocks, on a Caribbean beach. You need to use your breathing, like being in labour. Seeing how I was struggling, even with a hand and paddle, Tara gave me the gentlest of taps with the cane. David complained that it looked faked, and that he needed some stripes. Almost in tears on my behalf – she really is the sweetest of girls – she gave me six corking blows across my backside. How I howled, and danced, and wished I were dead. I couldn't believe anyone would pay for this insanity.

Over lunch Tara told me that she worked as a pro-domme, explained where she advertised, how she kept up her online profile, how much money she made, and how much she enjoyed herself. Some of her clients had become friends, she said. It was a privilege to be allowed to be part of someone else's fantasy, to bring their dreams to life; it was engaging and creatively fulfilling, a dawn to dusk delight.

Or quite possibly she didn't say any of that. It sounds more like the kind of thing I'd say, to be honest. And this is 12 years ago now, so I don't really remember anything she said, only that it sounded enticing, and well-paid. Two daughters at boarding school! That's, what, £60 grand a year or so? That was me sold. I love spanking, but I love money even more. On the long drive home, bottom throbbing, brain buzzing, I made a plan. Aged 30, I'd swop my g-string for a riding crop.

I set up a profile on ITC, an online site devoted to spanking, chiefly of the domestic variety – ITC stands for In The Corner. Most women had pictures alongside their ads, but I didn't want to show my face, and didn't have anyone to help me take a picture of some random, anonymous body part – boot heel, or leather clad bottom – so I stuck to text, and kept it simple. Elegant, educated disciplinarian seeks like-minded individuals to train and, where necessary, punish. Something like that. I decided less was more, and anyway, I didn't have a clue what I was doing or what would seem enticing. Plenty of girls seemed to reference their vast array of outfits, implements, experience at role-play: I didn't have any of that to boast about. In fact, I quickly realised getting a set of implements together had to be my first priority. Slippers and hairbrushes would be easy and cheap; canes and leather paddles, jolly expensive, the good ones at least, and how many would I need? Some girls posed beside collections of hundreds. I decided to buy one heavy leather strap, and one cane, both pretty cheap, and hope that my first clients were either too innocent and inexperienced to care, or very experienced and good enough to give me some direction as to what I needed and where to shop.

They would come to my house, I decided. I didn't much like the idea – a two-up two-down end terrace Victorian cottage, with thin walls and nosy neighbours, but what choice did I have? I'd have to say I was involved with a lot of noisy building projects, all of them necessitating a stream of men, a lot of loud thwacking sounds, and the occasional scream. Obviously they wouldn't believe me, but equally obviously I cared about money more than I cared about reputation, or I wouldn't already have been a sex worker 12 years. I had a spare room, painted an unfortunate shade of cheery yellow. Never mind: I'd close the curtains, and perhaps it would look a more sinister mustard shade. I carted up a wooden chair and coffee table, which might just possibly do for a desk, if you squinted, and were very short. I so hate spending money, and didn't want to go spending out on school desks and the like before I knew if I could really do this, or indeed, if I would get any interest.

Of the last point, at least, it rapidly became apparent there was no doubt. Five minutes after the advertisement went live, my inbox was flooded. Men do love a new girl, and by making myself so mysterious, I'd inadvertently piqued their interest all the more. I'd answer one email, and another five would appear in its place. Enquiry after enquiry, questions I didn't have the answer to, in the main, questions I now know are largely wank fodder – What exactly will you do to me? Have you always been into spanking? Were you spanked as a child? How hard can you spank? What's your ideal scenario? Do you have a cap and gown? What will you do if you find I'm wearing frilly knickers? Get an erection? Do you punish the hands? Are you an accurate caner? How hard can you cane? And on, and on. I bluffed as much as I dared, and tried my very best to give thoughtful answers to each, at least at the start. I decided to take a strict, scolding, no nonsense, threatening tone, but this didn't suit my style at all, and proved quite exhausting, so I soon returned to my usual chatty, friendly self. They responded to this better, and kept writing. I emailed until my back and fingers groaned, and soon realised I wasn't getting much closer to making any actual money. They loved the chat, but were less keen to make an actual appointment, or talk cash. I planned to ask £100 an hour, which seemed, from my brief foray into the subject, pretty well average. It was £70 for a strippergram and they're only ten minutes long, but I had to pay an agent and drive to them.

Ah, if only I'd had a mentor to guide me through! Less of the chat, more business; no more than three emails until an actual appointment is made; no endless great descriptive screeds – it's a waste of your time and you won't earn a penny from it; they'll add your thoughts to their wank bank and jog on. I knew nothing. I wore myself out trying to be accommodating. But subs will take and take if you let them. They're greedy for your time and attention, endlessly fascinated by the subject of spanking, every tiny nuance. Finally – finally – I got a sensible email from a John (they are, by and large, all called John, or Peter), who fancied being my first, and had a time and date in mind. It suited me. Suddenly this had become real. It was happening. Terrified, I logged off and rested my head gingerly on my desk. A real live pervert knew where I lived, and he planned to visit me next week. Jesus. I'd dealt with perverts all my working life, but they'd always been in pubs and clubs, or occasionally their houses or workplaces for strippergrams. Never my home. Could I really do this?

Well of course I could. Some piss-poor memoir this would be if I couldn't. My new friend Tara did it all day long, and made a fortune. Clearly I'd identified that the service I was offering was popular and needed; surely I could make a killing too, without being killed myself. Just the first one would be a bit traumatic and weird, no doubt, but no worse than the first time you rip your knickers off in a club. I was young, and brave, and greedy. Anyway, I'd ordered a cane. Damned if I was gonna waste that tenner.

The cane and strap came discreetly wrapped in a poster tube. Excited, I ripped it open and gave myself a few practise swots on the hands and thighs – Jesus, they hurt, but that's was splendid; that's what they were paying for, after all, and it wouldn't be me that would suffer it. Then I placed a cushion on a chair and practised whacking. I learned to line up the implement and give a few practise taps in the right place first, like a golfer, before properly letting rip: to bend the knees, swing from the hips, raise the beast high above my shoulder, and bring it down without twatting the lampshade. At least, I did after a few goes.

John turned up around 6 p.m. a couple of days later. I liked the sound of John, felt confident he wasn't a psychopath, yet still had my mother hiding in my bedroom with a baseball bat, just in case. I also had a few glasses of wine to ready my nerves, possibly an error given how hard and how accurately he insisted he be caned. I decided to smile and style my way through, and only stumbled very slightly when the doorbell rang.

Instantly, my first spankee set me at my ease. He was an old hand, was John. He'd seen everyone and done it all. In his 60s, just recovering from some scary heart operation – the whole of his torso tattooed with a jagged purple scar – he spent most of his hour giving me a tutorial on my new business, explaining the tools I desperately needed, the positions most often requested, the idiots best avoided, and paying me for the privilege. He let me practise my few pathetic implements on his backside – "Bit to the left, avoid the whipround, that's it…"

The sub is always in charge. Play all you like with the twin heady rushes of power and control: under it all the sub is having things to him, and therefore he dictates the terms. Obviously exploring that rather ruins playtime, so have those conversations beforehand. In a professional setting, I like to do it by email first – previous experience, whether they can be marked, implement/position preference, hard limits. This isn't 'topping from the bottom'; it's gracious good sense and manners. You have to establish trust before you can relax into having terrifying, painful things done to you. Otherwise they remain simply terrifying.

That was enough remembering for one day. I was of an age when I had more behind me than ahead, and you can't contemplate that for too many hours before becoming maudlin. Richard had gone with the smallest of nods. I went back to my husband. I'd a date to prepare for.

Chapter Fourteen

Turns out 8 a.m. is an exceedingly cold, dark, depressing time of day, and this particular 8 a.m. was enhanced by a heavy rainstorm, which I shuffled through in dumb rebellion. I'd worn stupid shoes that made my arse look great. Somehow turning up at this inconvenient time and location to meet a stranger seemed a reasonable means of punishing my husband, and for that reason only I persevered. See, Robert? See what you made me do? If only you were less of a dick I wouldn't have to stagger out of my marital bed and into the rain, risking smudged mascara and broken ankles, to seek validation from mystery men, would I now? I took pleasure in my discomfort, pinched toes, numb fingers, rain-splattered back.

St Agatha's wasn't much warmer than the street, but at least had a roof. I stood dripping in the porch, wringing out my idiotic red beret. Sheep must be permanently cold and damp. Wool is useless against the elements. Nice one, God. Was God here, waiting for the chance to save my soul? Didn't seem likely. I couldn't see him. Just a load of old women. People who come to church always seem to be those who have least reason for gratitude. Ugly, lumpen, crippled, misshapen, a sure sign to the rest of us that Jesus is the last resort, rather than a joyous life-affirming first prize. Where was this prick, anyway? Why wasn't he here waiting for me?

I read a poster about how few people in the world had access to indoor toilets. I suppose that's sad. Didn't seem to compare with my wet hair and numb toes. I can never understand how people can really be interested in stuff that isn't about them. Are they all just pretending? I stared at a stone wedged into the church wall. Matthew Tubbs, died 1835. Well, so what? What had it to do with me? Some rich fella pegs it, as we all must, and asked to have his stupid name graffitied in a church, and I'm meant to see it and care? Probably even Mrs Tubbs didn't care all that much. Probably a blessing to be rid of the vain prick. I shifted my weight from ankle to ankle. Red with a three-inch heel, since you ask. Rather too slutty for daywear, especially in a church, but this seemed like a date, or as close as I was likely to get, so I'd felt compelled to make the effort.

My husband, for instance, spends around 18 hours a day thinking about obscure 70s punk bands – Christ, maybe more, maybe he dreams of them too, what do I know? Well, but why? Does he imagine they think of him back? And what is there to think about? Some idiots decided to make some noise a few years ago: big deal. Is it going to make him any money? Get him talked about in important high-falutin quarters? Is it buggery. So why the bloody hell does he bother?

The enthusiasm with which other people approach life astounds me. Let's look at a stately home, they'll say; let's go to Italy! Let's see this play, that band! Am I seriously the only one buried in my own head, thinking – I'm not getting any attention here, there's not even the slightest chance of my getting laid, and yet this is meant to be a treat? Or worse those morons who get themselves snarled up over the state of the world. We'll all be dead soon, you idiots. What does it matter who's in charge when it happens or how long it takes? The idea of the world going on without me is deplorable. Let it burn up the minute I'm gone. Suits me. I'll take it as my rightful tribute.

Presumably all those other humans are trying urgently to distract themselves from their own futility, and yet they'd call me shallow. I tipped forward a little from the hips to show off taut buttocks, my womanly shape, pretending to admire Mr Tubbs' excellent engraving, fully aware that all eyes were on me. There, Matthew Tubbs, that's the most use you've been in a few years, maybe ever, you wretched old heap. You made a man stare at my arse. Maybe I could grow to like you.

Every old lump of humanity in the church looked ill. Red noses and streaming eyes abounded. I could feel a vague ache settling over my own flesh. How was I meant to recognise my artist?

When he walked in I knew at once of course. It wasn't a pleasant face, sour, sweaty, slightly bestial. He was overweight and not over tall, an unfortunate combination. His nostrils flared when he saw me. Narrow dark eyes seemed in this strange early light to be shot through with red. There was something repellent, animal, about his stare. I lowered my own gaze.

"Clara. What an unexpected treat." He bent to kiss my cheek. There was a careless scorn in the remark and kiss both and it took a beat for me to realise how much it hurt. I suddenly recognised how idiotic I must look, done up and damp at this hour for a bloody ugly stranger. I lifted my head.

"I keep my promises."

"I seriously doubt that. But I'm glad you're here." He turned to walk to the back of the church and beckoned me to follow. Sat in a pew and stared forward. I wedged in beside him, feeling his heavy tweed coat graze my hand, thinking: perhaps I do look ridiculous, but I don't care, I don't care, what this ugly creature thinks of me. He continued to stare forward. I stole a glance at his profile. Thick primitive lips, broad nose, small eyes, flabby features incongruously perched on scarf and tweed coat, like a gibbon in a suit. Apparently he didn't plan to speak.

"So now you've had a look at me, are you still interested in my modelling for you?"

"By all means."

"How flattering." Discreetly I pushed back a strand of wet hair behind an ear, smoothed down my eyebrows.

"Don't be flattered. Or at least, don't assume it's your looks I'm interested in. It isn't."

That hurt too, damn him. "What then? My scintillating personality? And you imagine you're artist enough to capture that, do you?"

"Yes. If you'll trust me enough to let me. You'll have to drop all pretences and let me get at the real you, then capture that. I imagine that could be interesting."

"For you."

"For everyone who sees it. I'm having an exhibition next month."

I was beginning to feel rather sick. The two pints of coffee I'd swallowed before I left were swirling alarmingly in my guts. I wished very passionately that he would look at me, rather than the suspended Christ on which his eyes seemed to dwell. Damp and middle-aged I might be, but surely I didn't cut such a poor figure as that.

"Will I be naked?"

"You'd prefer that, wouldn't you? Nothing conceals like nudity. I'll leave that up to you. It will chiefly be portraits anyway." My hand felt warm where his sleeve had grazed it. I wanted him to go away so I could think about him. Then realised this was his space and I was intruding in it.

"Shall we meet at your studio then? Next time. If you feel comfortable I'm not a murderer."

"Sorry? Yes. I don't, incidentally. But I don't much care whether you murder me or not. Here's my card. Come tomorrow morning, if you like. Don't wear so much makeup. It doesn't suit you."

"Goodbye then."

"What? Yes. goodbye."

Standing made me remember how my toes hurt and how much I'd been looking forward to this encounter for reasons that now seemed totally mysterious. "What the bloody hell are you looking at, anyway?"

He gestured at the torn teary Christ on the cross. "Beautiful, isn't he? Can't you identity?"

I stared at the gouged holes in the hands and feet, the face contorted with pain, and remembered my RE teacher telling me how, in that position, he would slowly have suffocated to death.

"Identify? How?"

"With the suffering. Being forced to endure the unendurable. Not like tragic heroes of Shakespeare, say, who contain some flaw which brings about their own downfall. But suffering purely and keenly only because God or fate has decreed it."

"I certainly understand making the best use of suffering. Using it to give life meaning and flavour. Is that what you mean?"

His eyes drifted to my face. They were indeed shot through with red, as if he'd been crying, or smoked a ton of weed. It gave his gaze an animal glow.

"No. You know about suffering as a playful, indulgent, bourgeois act. I mean suffering undertaken indifferently, because one must."

God help me, I tried to understand. I sat beside him again and thought about Christ. And my own suffering, such as it was. Of course I could make myself cry by ruminating on the men who'd broken their promises and scarpered, or being a powerless child, but why the hell would I? Enough to get through each day. Repress, suppress, look forward.

"No. I'm no martyr. I suspect you may be."

"Martyr? In the old sense or the new? In the new sense, if I exude a sense of moral superiority it's deserved and intended, but that's not what I meant. I wouldn't die for my beliefs. I don't even have any beliefs. The crucial part of the Christ narrative is the resurrection. The suffering isn't the end. It's a part of the process, but not the final chapter. It's the Good Friday before Easter Sunday. If you can't identify I envy you. One suffers, but one comes out fresh the other side."

"Not if you suffocate. Unless you have supernatural powers."

"Hmm? Well, no. Quite. One must be cautious. But without the redemption the suffering is futile. I can't bear that idea. That one should go through all this for no reason. It must have meaning."

"Do you expect your thwarted love life to start a new religion?"

He smiled at that, or at least twisted his face into a new shape. "No. But the chance to identify with that violence – to confront it, to grasp it – it's a way, paradoxically, to escape from it, in one's own life."

"Yes. Using suffering to explore and create and move to the other side. I do understand that. It's the opposite of martyrdom. You want to leave suffering behind and move to the next experience."

"I do. I very much do." Jesus had lost his lustre; his eyes were on mine. I wondered if he might try to kiss me, and what I'd do if he did. To delay the quandary I kept talking.

"You need suffering to be witnessed, though, or it ceases to possess reason. Depersonalised objective pain cannot be tolerated. You need to be linked to another person while you suffer or it has no meaning. That I do understand.""That's how you earn a living."

"Exactly."

"Although your husband thinks you don't."

"Yes."

"Then who witnesses your suffering, if the people closest to you, your family, know nothing about you?"

I shrugged. "No one. I guess."

"Then it has no meaning and is therefore, by definition, we've agreed, intolerable."

"I don't think about it like that."

"Strikes me you don't think about anything very much. Probably wise. But if you're going to pose for me, if that's really what you want, you need to start thinking. And then you may find you need to meditate on Christ as a potent symbol for what you're going through. You complain, you manoeuvre futilely, it makes no difference. You just have to endure it. And when you have, you feel rejuvenated. Like Saint Sebastian, who found himself more filled with love the more he was pierced with arrows."

The word love had brought the conversation back to the personal and made me hope this may not have been an utterly wasted morning. "It was your idea, I'll remind you. My modelling for you. You make it sound a riot and a half. Who witnesses your suffering, eh? Random sex workers you find on the internet?"

"Nobody. Nobody sees me. I live trying to find someone to see me. I can only survive knowing how much life there is in me, and how much I have to lose if the suffering is meaningless. I keep trying. I really do." My urge to be his one, the one who could see and understand, must have been exactly what he was counting upon. The urge to rescue and redeem is strong in some girls, me included. God knows why. It's been the downfall of many, and usually the best of girls too. I stood up again.

"Well. Allow me to wish you the best of luck in your quest. I have a 10 a.m. suffering to inflict, so I'd better crack on. Happy cogitating."

I looked back once at the church door to see his eyes locked on the hanging Christ. When the door slammed I was already counting the hours to our next encounter, and planning my outfit.

Chapter Fifteen

I could smell Richard beside me, fresh sweat and booze. A companionable smell. He was pecking out top tips for young journalists, although he appeared to have omitted the most crucial piece of advice: be born to wealthy, indulgent parents. I thought about pointing that out, but he seemed grumpy already. Fine. I could advise young people too. I had heaps of useful pointers to share, no privilege necessary. And a day to get through before the shoot.

Advice to girls who'd like to turn pro-domme

Over the last 12 years I have tried to help at least 20 girls become pro-dommes, and none of them have succeeded. And yet it's the easiest business imaginable to start and run. You need a strap and a cane and an email address, that's all. Get a few basics right and the money will come flooding in, more than you can spend.

Girls tend often to be discouraged by the number of idiots they encounter in the early days. Subs love a new girl. They will flock to your Twitter, shower you with questions and compliments, but never think of giving you any money. They are often needy and greedy, obsessive monomaniacs; they'll gladly and recklessly spend every moment of every day talking to you about spanking, if you let them. If you're obsessed with spanking too, fine, chat back. But if you're in this to earn a living, you have to learn to answer only 1 in 50 of their messages. Quickly you'll learn from the tone and language who is wasting your time, and who, conversely, is planning to give you any money. Look for practical, tightly focussed correspondence, along the lines of, when are you free, what do you charge, do you have a fluffy pink cardigan like my aunt Agatha used to wear (photo attached)? These are very good signs that a visit is a distinct possibility. Those boys are out there. They're not all wretched timewasters. But some days, particularly at the beginning, the good ones can be hard to find among the dross.

Bad correspondence will be vague, fanciful, long-winded. How hard would you spank me, Miss, is my own personal pet hate. Bloody well pay me and you'll find out, dick weasel. Or, how would you tie me down; you're so sexy and beautiful; does this turn you on; were you spanked as a child; would you like to hear what happened to me at school once; here's a picture of what happened to my dick when I watched you cane that girl. All these chaps can safely be ignored. Don't worry that you're being rude. I assure you, they're accustomed to it. They're being rude by wasting your time. You're running a business. Time is money. Spend it wisely.

I don't socialise with clients. Plenty of girls do, get taken for dinner and cocktails and theatre trips: I do not. I'm selling my time, and I don't care if I'm figging you, caning you or drinking champagne with you: it still costs. This sounds harsh, I realise, but otherwise you risk blurring the boundaries, and once you've done that, it's impossible to get a relationship back on a business footing. I'm not your friend. I'm not your girlfriend. I'm your domme, and I cost £120 an hour. Chap I see likes to be caned, then take me for lunch, then be caned after lunch. He pays for three hours of my time: I charge for the time spent eating as well as caning. The true sub will understand and respect that. There are many of my clients of whom I'm extremely fond and would count among my closest friends. I've supported them through the deaths of their parents and the births of their grandchildren, through health crises and marital discord; I've held them when they've sobbed, and felt glad and privileged to do it... but it still always cost them.

If you feel awkward turning down champagne and a night at the theatre, invent a jealous husband who makes these tedious rules and will cheerfully cripple them if they disobey.

I've said you need only a strap, a cane and an email, and that's true, but some other stuff is handy too. Choose a name that's really easy to spell – men are often quite stupid when they're horny. Get yourself on PurplePort and have some decent photographs taken. There are 100s of keen photographers and filmmakers out there desperate to expand their portfolios; some of them will even pay you, but on no account should you pay them. Then get yourself on Twitter and Instagram. Facebook is a waste of your time. I am on Fetlife, but I've always found that to be a terrible irritating bother too, and I don't think I've ever made a penny from it. Twitter is where it all happens for me. Twitter users seem more savvy and interesting. Post every day to keep yourself fresh in people's minds. Try to find some way to make yourself stand out. Don't try to be pretend to be something you're not; it quickly grows wearisome, and worse, obvious. I tried to pretend I was this stern angry leather clad sex goddess at the start, but in truth I'm clever, kinky and maternal, and that's fine too. That'll sell. Whatever you are, you'll be wanted. You'll find your place, and heaps of men to desire and worship you there. Enjoy their adoration: you've earned it, it belongs to you.

Don't worry too much about getting zillions of implements and outfits at the start. People will give you heaps of things, suggest things, make recommendations as to what they like. A good cane is a necessity (Quality Control, for preference: expensive, yes, but it will outlast you, and anything cheaper is likely to break on its third outing); so is a decent strap, but otherwise you can find stuff around your house to start you off – slippers, hairbrushes, wooden spoons, belts, fish slices, fly swots, rulers. There's much to be said for a hand-spanking as well, intimate, sensuous and convenient. If, like me, you plan to specialise in domestic discipline, a pencil skirt, seamed stockings, silky blouses and heels are essential, and probably a fine array of colourful cardigans too: think 1950s headmistress. If you're planning to move more down the BDSM route, you're on your own. Leather caps and boots and tattoos and piercings wouldn't work for me. Not with my accent and demeanour. Figure out your USP and dress accordingly. What do you like? What do you look like? What do you sound like? Who's responding to your advertisements?

I don't advertise now, but when I did, itc-mag.co.uk was the original and best, and they haven't paid me to say so. It costs £1 a week to place your ad on there, like a newsagent's window. I warn you, when you start, you'll be inundated. You'll spend days sifting through hundreds of replies wondering what on earth you've got yourself into. Persevere. Gradually it will all start to assume an order and make a sort of sense. Add other dommes on Twitter: there's a supportive, friendly community out there, and if you're not sure about a fella, ask: if he's weird doubtless one of us will know about it.

Ooh, actually, one more crucial piece of kit is a notebook. Write down your clients' preferences – over the knee (OTK), touching toes, draped over your desk, wood, leather; any key words he likes to hear – some will go wild for the phrase "smacked bottom" or "slap" or "now you're starting to learn your lesson"; some insist on pearl earrings, plimsolls, pink stockings, whatever. Write down how many cane strokes they took on your last encounter too, and how they like their tea, the names of their grandchildren or dog, and whether or not they can be marked. They'll be overjoyed on their next visit to discover how well you've remembered their predilections.

I read once that you'll never get rich if you don't make money while you sleep, and this seemed such an interesting idea I've set up a fair few sidelines in consequence. I sell erotic novels on Amazon, clips on Clips4sale, and I'm on Onlyfans too. It's a real treat to wake up and find your bank account has swelled while you were snoring.

And if I sound mercenary – well, I am. I come from desperate poverty and I'll do anything, anything, to avoid a return to it. This takes nothing from the fact that I love my job, love spanking, love my brave, fascinating clients.

Have fun.

"Tell me something interesting," Richard said. "I'm bored to blazes."

"I met someone in a church I think might actually be Satan, and I suspect I'm going to be unfaithful to my husband."

"Excellent. A punter?"

"Photographer."

"Same difference, surely. Is it childhood conditioning, or being derived from degenerate stock, that turned you into such a loathsome slut?"

"The combination, I imagine. Usually it helps me get what I want. Doesn't seem to be working recently."

"Perhaps you've got too old and pathetic and haggard with booze to pull those tricks any longer."

"Perhaps. Although usually the older one gets, the more efficiently they work."

"Would it matter, to anyone, you being unfaithful?"

"I feel there's something significant about this one."

"What sort of significant?"

"He" – I hesitated to say the words, realising how pathetic they would sound in this place, to those ears. "He seems to understand me. To see me."

"Well, you're hardly complex. This is boring me too. Tell me something interesting that he told you."

"That he identifies with Christ. That suffering can only be meaningful if it's witnessed and worked through."

"Doesn't sound exactly Satanic."

"It was how he said it. Like a threat."

Richard reached under the table for a smuggled homemade sandwich while he contemplated this news. Cheddar and coleslaw, slimy with age.

"Well. Sounds like it might make an interesting blog post, anyway. Does anyone read them?"

"Dunno, honestly. Not much, probably. The more devoted stalkers tell me I'm amazing, but then they also buy jars of my piss, so I don't know I feel particularly validated by their critiques."

"You can write."

"Yeah, I know. Thanks though."

"I mean, you can tell a story."

"Thank you. That means a lot."

"I bet you could do something else, you know, if you wanted."

I sighed. "So you said. But I couldn't, sweetie. I'm not the right sort to accomplish anything. It's not enough to be talented and clever and hardworking, you have to know the right people and the right things to say and all that. And I don't, and I never will."

"I bet you could learn."

"No I couldn't, because it's innate, or damn near. That confidence, that sense of entitlement. Alongside the parents that ease your way, send you to the right schools, introduce you to the right people. I was bound to be disappointed before I was born. Like you were born to succeed."

"Actually I'm from quite a modest background."

"Oh, actually, are you?"

"Yes." He went back to typing. I sat listening to the quickening drumming of my own heart. I didn't believe that. You can smell it coming off them. Him. You can. Fine. Bollocks to you then.

He slammed his laptop shut and made me jump. "You know, my dad couldn't actually even read."

"No?"

"No."

"Well. I didn't even have a dad, you privileged wanker."

He beamed at me. "Mine beat me every night."

"Oh, the joy of instilling such passion in a man so young! No wonder you've accomplished so much."

"You're fucking insufferable and I'm going for a piss."

"Fascinating. Get me some crisps, posh boy."

I took advantage of his absence to check Facebook and Twitter and every other timewaster going. I admired the man's work ethic but didn't quite find myself equal to it. He was probably doing the same in the loo. Alex was dishing out sausage rolls to asylum seekers, very noisily. A bag of Wotsits came at my head.

"Thank you!"

"You're very welcome."

"Just look at this prick, now."

"Handsome chap."

"It's basking in the warm glow of feeling worthwhile and necessary."

"What's wrong with that?"

"A desire to make yourself feel better at the expense of the vulnerable? Seeking power by patronising the weak and needy? At least give it its proper name. It's a kink. And the urge to help emerges from the same place as the urge to exploit."

"Don't you think maybe he and – um –"

"Karen."

"Yes, her, just can't bear the idea of people suffering, and so they feel compelled to do something practical to help?"

"No. Because they don't want the suffering to end. They'd be horrified. Where would they get their kicks them? Where find the thrills that give life its particular zest? There's plenty of unglamorous, untrendy suffering here to be ameliorated, but they don't fancy that. Like I say, he could have just not been a cock."

I turned up the volume. They had written a song. She played the ukulele. Of course. Alex on guitar. Me and my sodding passion for musicians.

"The Tory boys picnic!"

"Actually, that's quite good."

"They're raising money for BLM training so they can understand how unintentionally racist and exploitative they are. Guilt, repentance, restitution. It's the old story. The thrill of sin and forgiveness. Weirdos who don't know they're weirdos are the most infuriating. Just – you know."

"Own it?"

"I hate that expression, but well, yeah."

"So how should aid be distributed? Or should they just be left to die?"

"I don't know. No, of course not. Probably by ballot, like jury service. But certainly people who seek to help the needy should be let nowhere near the needy. Surely they're suffering enough."

"Like the way people who want to be politicians should never be allowed to be politicians."

"Exactly."

"My wife is a Lib Dem councillor."

"Oh Jesus Christ. I'm sorry. Ex-wife, surely."

"Yes, ex-wife. There were a lot of committees."

"Cheese and wine parties, pub quizzes?"

"Yup. Open mics. Choirs, ceilidhs."

"You poor bastard. She's still got the kids?"

"Oh yes, of course."

"See much of them?"

"Every other weekend. Classic. I'd best get on."

"Yeah, me too. Why don't you work at home?"

"And miss your pathetic haggard old face and charming Satanic anecdotes? Why don't you?"

"Husband no 2 keeps wanting me to listen to his recent compositions until I start fantasising about having a stroke just to stop the talking. Presumably you have the opposite problem."

"I write better among other humans. It's too easy to distract yourself home alone. Plus it all gets woven in, snatches of chat, outfits, smells. All meat to the sausage machine. Which is calling. Sorry. Deadline."

"No, no, fair."

I reached for my glass, gleefully anticipating that delightful moment when the wine hits the brain and nothing mattered. Developing an interest in emotionally unavailable men is just another form of masochism. Like horror films, hot curries, caning, abseiling. An urge to feel something intense, not be sick and bored of your own dreary yourself. I knew all about that. Where was I? Ah yes. Hard limits.

Hard limits are those which, no matter how horny or drunk or warmed up you might be, you have no interest in pursuing. Soft limits are more flexible – the cane, for example, terrifies me, like most sensible folk, but sometimes after a long exciting session I can withstand it, even want it. The good top knows when no means no, and also when it means maybe.

So with every top tip that follows, bear that in mind. All bottoms are different and beautiful. Respect their preferences and needs, for their sake and yours:

Hand-spanking and short implements – brushes, slippers, paddles

… and other such beasts you can use OTK. When using your hand, cup it, as if you were trying to catch raindrops. This will hurt you less and them more, and make a pleasant ringing sound too. So much of the pleasure of thrashing is auditory, I find. The sound of a belt being removed and snapped fair near makes me come on the spot.

Alternate cheeks to begin, then move to half a dozen on one, then the other. Play about with tempo and positioning of the smack – avoiding anything above the coccyx: protect the kidneys: but feel free to move down the thighs, although using only about a quarter of the force you apply to the buttocks: thighs are tender beasts. Put your shoulder into it. Don't be lazy. Nothing worse than a gentle pat, the sort you might use to reward a chihuahua. The sound should ring in the ears.

Keep them guessing – add in the odd rub and stroke to give them a breather, then resume your efforts with greater intensity. Interweave a leg about theirs so they feel they can't escape. Place your other hand on the small of their back for comfort and stability, or occasionally use both hands. If it's a playful scene, add some games – have them watch a clock while you give them as many thwacks as you can in a minute, get them singing Nellie the Elephant while you keep time on their buttocks, like a pervy rhythm section. Chap I see likes to get himself into the wheelbarrow position across my lap, then play Donna Summer's 'I Feel Love' while I bongo him to the beat, going double handed at the crazy midway disco instrumental. That's jolly good fun.

Add ice cubes, kisses or blow on the reddened area during or after. Or deep heat if you're feeling mean. Move your fingernails delicately over the sore spots and enjoy the lines you can make in the newly reddened area.

Canes, tawses, floggers and other long implements

Stand back. Stand much further back than you think you need to, then further back still. Line up your shot with a few taps first, as if you were playing golf. If you are right-handed, aim entirely for the left buttock. Trust me on this: the right will take care of itself. If you aim for the right you'll get "whip round," the beast bouncing around the hip or torso, which is exceedingly painful and unpleasant, resulting in marks that will take months to heal, and show you up for an amateur.

Aim for accuracy before intensity. Practise on a cushion or sofa arm first, and when you graduate to a human, consider cushioning their lower back and thighs with some belted-on pillows, so only the buttocks are revealed. At least to begin, place the spankee in the position you find easiest – often having the subject lie flat out on his stomach is easiest for the amateur caner. This allows gravity to assist you, and there's no need to worry about angles.

It's vastly easier to cane on the bare. Pants or trousers tend to encourage the cane to skip off in an unexpected direction. Be brave. Sink your cane into naked flesh. The resultant stripes are exquisite. Enjoy them. You've earned them. Both of you.

Once you've got in your hand-eye coordination (easier and speedier if you're a tennis or hockey player) give it some real welly. Bring your shoulder right back. Do it with conviction. Have confidence. Tops need to assume authority and expertise, even when they're far from feeling it. Then practise and practise: there's no substitute for it. Plenty of chaps will be keen to help you learn.

One you've established the basics, mess about with position and speed. Dishing out two swift strokes of the cane, without giving the sub time to catch his breath, is a thrilling, devilish trick. Having him bend right over, on a horse or touching his toes, will also make the sensation more intense: the skin is pulled tauter in these positions.

Thinner, whippier canes are more stingy; thicker, more thuddy. It seems counterintuitive, but often the thicker ones are less painful, easier to withstand, as well as easier to control. Obviously shorter ones are generally easier for the top. But again, experiment. Don't buy cheap: they'll break the first time you put any force into it. Some people swear by soaking them in oil or water, but I've never bothered. I suppose it might add to the density. But if you start with good canes you'll find they don't need much looking after, the way real gold won't tarnish.

The cane may also be applied to the breasts, the thighs, the anus, if you are very accurate; the hands, or the feet, which is known as bastinado. For me, nothing beats a bottom. But experiment. Feet can be useful if a chap can't be marked. Only the most suspicious wives will go inspecting their husband's soles.

I'm a traditionalist, so six, or twelve, or multiples thereof for me. Leave decimalisation to the continentals.

I don't use safe words. Never have. I believe a good top should be able accurately to assess when a bottom has had his fill, from the squirms and the sobs and the sighs. For me it would ruin the play if the sub possessed means to make it stop. If you find you just have to endure it, then very frequently you do. If I am going to be powerless, let me be utterly powerless; otherwise the knowledge I could choose to make it stop at any point makes the whole experience seem a bit silly. I wouldn't play with anyone I don't trust to know when I'd had enough. But if you prefer the idea of retaining some measure of control, I won't judge you, or at least only a little bit, in a way you'll likely find alluring.

"Another?"

I looked at my watch. "Make it a gin this time, would you?"

"Of course."

"Trust fund payout, is it? I'm kidding! You're a darling." I saluted, then blew him a kiss.

Role-play

A chap contacted me a few years back asking if he could book a session – and if possible, could he bring some 18th century outfits for us both? Oh, and a makeshift stile? Well, of course he could. Surely a delightful afternoon beckoned. He wanted to be transformed into a Georgian member of the gentry, out walking with his fiancée (whose name, I recall, had to be Alice), when by some mishap he got caught halfway over a stile, buttocks exposed, trousers caught tight on a nail. While he squirmed, begged and remonstrated by turn, naughty Alice chose to spank him, birch him, belt him, take a hairbrush to him, and for the finale, fig him. Quite where Alice found a piece of root ginger in the English countryside wasn't fully addressed in the narrative. Maybe they were carrying a picnic.

That was one of the most elaborate, exciting role-plays I've ever engaged in. For two hours I was Alice, and I went home giddy with her teasing cheek. He'd made furniture to accompany it, for heaven's sake, and spent a fortune on glorious, authentic outfits, which instantly transported us into a new, playful mindset.

More usually I'm a strict aunt, boss, wife, mother-in-law, prison officer, member of a socialist revolutionary kidnapping collective, but most commonly, of course, teacher. I can drop into my "Now, you know the rules here, and also the consequence for breaking them – you've let the school down very badly – I've half a mind to tell your parents" patter in my sleep. In films, in sessions, in away days, school scenes are hard wired into the British psyche. Education-based role-plays probably account for 50% of all my sessions. School scenes are, to my knowledge, the only role-play scenarios that have whole buildings and days devoted to them. I'm deputy headmistress at Whipstock Grange now, which usually has around eight to ten naughty pupils at its school sessions; if you like your discipline with a side order of striped ties and stationery, I can wholeheartedly recommend it. Some bright spark calculated I must have delivered around 1300 strokes of the cane on my last appearance: small wonder I drove home half asleep.

Role-play is a crucial element of BDSM and CP, akin to the value of fantasy to masturbation. Turning pain to pleasure involves a mind trick of some description, or it remains simply pain, which is horrid and to be avoided. To seek it out, to want to inflict it, there must be a reason. Very frequently people fall back on stories to explain their need to themselves, and not only in BDSM: we all live and die by the metaphors we choose to inhabit. Fortunately, and unsurprisingly, masochists are inevitably clever, imaginative people. They need to be.

Incidentally, people outside the scene tend to assume that masochists pick sadists to play with: why wouldn't they? It's such a neat, obvious fit. In truth, only masochists tend to have the imagination and sensitivity to make a scene work; they want to please the other party, whichever role they happen to be assuming. Sadists don't like to be told what to do. They want things their way, all the time, and while it's fun to role-play that idea, in real life it quickly becomes rather wearisome, as anyone who's spent time with a toddler can testify. For a scene to be mutually satisfying and engaging, both parties must have imagination and empathy, and equal power when deciding on the rules.

Whether you're exploring stories with a play partner or a client, rules are crucial – i.e. any places you definitely don't want to go, or definitely must, for the story to work. Once I'm in role I don't come out of character, unless something very unexpected and untoward happens – a neighbours starts banging angrily on the door to say my 'guest' had blocked his drive with his car, for instance, as happened recently, and could he jolly well get out here and move it. This is the time to admit he is no longer Jenkins of 3B, caught watching the girls change for hockey practise, but Dave with the silver BMW, who'll have it keyed if he doesn't get his pants back on stat.

But otherwise, stay in role. Trust to the story. If you're with somebody inexperienced and they start giggling and making fatuous remarks, punish them for it. Let them know you're serious. They will thank you for it afterwards. Remember:

they want this. They want it to be authentic, to hurt, to be something they feel they can't escape. Honour that.

I love role-plays that start the second I open the door. Often a chap produces a note from his mother or teacher which gives me something to work with. "Ah, William, your mother says she caught you scrumping in my back garden and insists I deal with you…in any way I see fit." Or a chap who played an estate agent coming to value my house, who made several derogatory remarks about the state it was in, until I, incensed, threatened to tell his boss, unless…

There's no script. It's all improvised. Sometimes there might be some key phrases they want to hear, but usually you take an idea and run with it. I've done some acting, so I'm accustomed to that and relish the creative challenge. If you haven't, I'd say relax, and commit to the story. Give it the authority to take you wherever it wants. If you relax the other participant will relax. If you're in charge – whatever 'in charge' might mean in this particular scene – that's your job.

I find it easier to role-play with a client than a lover. In a relationship I inevitably assume the submissive role; my urge to please subsumes all else, so taking charge feels unnatural and awkward. It's easier to role-play brutal, impersonal indifference with a stranger. I need to work on that, and I'd be really interested to hear how anyone else has managed to overcome that challenge.

In any and all role-play, outfits count. We all love to dress up. I had a treasured dressing up box as a kid, and how privileged I am to possess a still more elaborate kit now I'm in my forties. Changing for a session promptly lifts you away from the workaday, helps you inhabit another character, whether girl guide, high court judge or correction officer. When I slip on my seamed stockings, pencil skirt, silk blouse, court shoes, I promptly become Clara. My patterns of speech become more elaborate, my stance more dominant; I move and speak in a way that automatically conveys – and moreover, demands – total respect. Playfulness is a crucial component of this fetish, and being elevated away from the real world, set soaring away into the realms of daydream and make believe ("I'm away to La La Land!" my friend Miss Prim would cry, as she opened the door to her dungeon), is one of its greatest rewards.

Having said that, around 20% of my sessions feature no role-play at all. We chat about art, books, family, politics, the benefits of leather over wood, while I whack. That's fun too. There's often something rather thrilling about pursuing the kind of conversation one might enjoy with one's maiden aunt while simultaneously walloping the bejesus out of someone: hearing him try to make his point about Brexit as I yank at his nipples or torture his inner thighs with my riding crop. The incongruity can add to the joy.

I admire the chaps who can take a real life hurt or humiliation and bring it to role-play, to own and explore in safety, like those chaps, surprisingly abundant in the scene, who want to be humiliated for having a tiny penis. For God's sake don't spoil their fun by telling them, but many of them are actually fairly average, in truth: still, clearly someone has mocked their manhood at some point, so that they seek to deal with the pain by controlling and eroticising it. People who can laugh at their own shortcomings no longer fear criticism, for it amuses, or better yet, arouses them, and heavens, what a skill! Similarly, I admire those who want to be racially abused in sessions – how incredibly liberating that must be! Personally I don't find myself equal to doing it – racial abuse is on a very short list of hard limits for me – but still, what a way to process a perceived power imbalance: paying a domme to explore it with you, take it to its ultimate limit, find it erotic, thrilling, then walk away from it. What a coup, what a skill, to make racism work for you!

A few chaps want to explore real life misdemeanours, for which they were never caught, never properly punished, the guilt for which has often haunted them over the years. I've punished some for drink-driving, for lying and cheating, recklessly endangering people's lives and happiness: often they want to be taken beyond their limits, properly thrashed in a way that will truly hurt them, seeking release in tears the way most masochists seek release in orgasm. I am not troubled by guilt, myself, so in these instances feel myself delving into deep and murky waters for which I'm profoundly unqualified, armed as I am with only a dozen canes and a yearning for a jolly caper. But I do my best. I have brought men to tears, probing at their deepest shame while beating them until they scream, but I don't seek these sessions out. For me, discipline is about play. It's an escape into fantasy, dressing up and larking about: a journey away from torment, not through it.

There is a potential pitfall to this starting the role-play the second you open the door idea: I did get the wrong fella once. Chap knocked on the door at precisely the most inopportune moment. Early 20s, handsome, slightly nervous looking: I thought I was in for a very happy hour.

"Right, you. Upstairs this minute." I said. He looked a bit surprised but did as he was told. I ushered him into my study and sat down.

"Jenkins, I'm sure you can guess why you're here. Your form tutor Miss Brown has explained that you were caught cheating in the maths exam –"

"What – what's going on?"

"Silence! Insolent boy! There is only one possible punishment for cheating at this school. As you're doubtless aware we are still firm believers here in corporeal punishment, and 12 cold hard strokes of the cane will be exactly the painful, humiliating shock you need to ensure you never try cheating again! Take down your trousers this minute."

"I only wanted to know if you wanted to change your broadband to Sky –"

"Don't be so ridiculous! Why would a schoolboy be interested in –" at which point there was another knock at the door and the penny dropped with a horrifying clang, right in the pit of my stomach.

"Oh. Balls. Crap. Um. Look, awfully sorry. Mistaken identity. Would you, um, mind hiding in the loo while I answer the door? Oh and, um, maybe not mentioning this to my neighbours, or, you know, anyone?"

The poor chap fled from my grip only too willingly. I let in the real Jenkins – late 60s, scrawny arsed, rather smug looking – and bid a sad adieu to the happy hour I'd imagined. As I passed the loo I said very loudly, "This way Jenkins – in here – I'll shut the door so we're not DISTURBED –" and bless him, the Sky seller took the hint, waiting to hear my door noisily slam before scampering down the stairs like a frightened rabbit. No one's ever tried to sell me Sky again. I probably went on a list.

I always used to work from my mum's house. She didn't mind. Quite enjoyed the fun. If I didn't know them or thought they sounded a bit weird she'd hide upstairs, but usually she'd trot off out. The chap who wanted to role-play as an estate agent opened her bedroom door unexpectedly and found her lying on the carpet doing sit ups. I'd do the same for her when she got a dodgy newbie – oh yes, she used to dommes too; I corrupted her about three years after I started. She got made redundant and thought, rather as I did all those years ago – why the hell not? It baffles me why more women don't think, why the hell not: so many seem to prefer dull and respectable to rich and fulfilled. Kinksters love the old girls. She earned more than me. To think I worried the sex industry would reject me when I hit 30! You can earn as long as you fancy. Occasionally we would offer double sessions. Cornered the market there, I can tell you.

Richard smiled at me as I slammed the laptop shut.

"All done?"

"For today, yeah. I dunno how you can stand sitting staring at a screen all day. It would drive me mental."

"You get used to it, like anything."

"Yeah, well. Enjoy the extra space. I've got an undertaker whose nappy needs changing, then home to make dinner. See you tomorrow?"

He raised his glass. "I'll be here from ten."

"Meh. I've got a photoshoot first thing. The Satanic weirdo. Save my place. And if I'm not here by noon, he's murdered me."

"Is it nearby? Do you want my number or anything? If I saved your life it would make for some quality copy. Dopey loathsome slut has life saved by handsome freelancer. Might even make the nationals."

I hesitated. "Nah. I'll be alright. Thanks though."

He shrugged, and got back to his baby journos.

"Bye then."

Chapter Sixteen

So I've stumbled into a few studios over the years, for various publications and films; and also for the amateur who hasn't a clue what he's doing, just fancies the thrill of having a naked girl before him, a shitty camera slung low to conceal his erection. John had all the gear, lights and backdrops, cases of lenses. He let me in wordlessly and beckoned me up the stairs. As directed, I was wearing much less makeup than usual, only enough to cover the worst of the scars, no lips or eyeliner, nothing to enhance. I felt dowdy and anxious without my war paint and suspected that was the plan. All the same, when I stood in front of the backdrop, watching him fiddle with his cameras, awaiting direction, I felt myself unravel. There's something soothing about being told exactly where to stand, how to look, which way your toes should curl. Liberates the mind. It's like self-inflicted bondage.

John lived in a four-storey house in the centre of town. Absurdly large for a solitary dweller, yet he certainly seemed to be the sole occupant. Pictures of women decorated the walls, largely naked, all looking vaguely distressed, and all, I noticed angrily, rather younger and thinner than me. This thought seemed beneath me, so I commanded it to vanish. With so many women of varying looks and ethnicities it was impossible to know where best to focus my jealous energy. Lots of dreadlocks, quite a few tattoos, all attached casually to the walls, butterflies rammed with steel. The place was clean and bare, arranged with prissy efficiency. I wondered if he might be gay, the parade of nipples an elaborate deceit. He offered wine and nothing else, and although it had just turned 9 a.m.

and my mouth was still a lively toothpastey tingle, I accepted hastily, and received a bucket of fruity chardonnay. He hadn't told me what clothing to remove, and I hadn't wanted to seem presumptuous, so slipped off only boots and socks. The floor was covered in white cloth. My glittery red toenails looked vulgar against it.

He'd dressed himself in designer jeans and shirt and smelled very powerfully of expensive aftershave. I couldn't decide if this was a seduction effort or further proof of his being gay, and my uncertainty on this score made me uneasy. If he were going to try to seduce me today – and on balance, this still seemed likeliest – I didn't want to feel unprepared for it. I watched his harsh, melancholy profile as he pointedly ignored me and busied himself with his gizmos. As he frowned over his light meters he pursed his lips, and I wondered how it would feel to kiss them. Probably a little like kissing a giraffe. Eventually he turned to stare at me, flabby features wrinkled with displeasure.

"Relax."

"I am relaxed."

"You couldn't look any less relaxed. You look like you're on the verge of a panic attack. Drink more wine, for God's sake. I haven't got all morning, if you have."

"Do you find shouting at women that they should relax generally encourages them to relax?"

"I don't really do encouragement. I'm used to being obeyed without question. Come and sit down for a bit." He perched on a tiny two-seater sofa and patted the seat beside him. I couldn't squeeze on to that without touching his thigh. I sat. He made a sudden grab for my right foot and began to massage it, sliding his soft fat fingers between my toes. I watched them snake over my skin, fascinated.

"Is that alright?"

"Yes," I said, since it seemed to be expected; then, hesitantly, "Thank you."

"You must be the most submissive dominatrix in town."

"It has been noted."

"Your USP."

"Wanting to please people is an asset in any line of work."

"Not for the artist."

"You must be very rich if that's honestly your philosophy."

"No one makes any money from art. If it's to possess truth it must please me. I don't give a damn who else it pleases."

"I must pretend to believe that myself when I go to work. But it's always the submissive who's truly in charge." His fingers were moving thickly between my toes, over the soles, with a pressure that was becoming painful.

"Not here it isn't. Do be quiet," he said, then lunged forward to grab my neck and thrust his tongue into my mouth. It probed with a flabby intensity somewhere between vile and thrilling. His fingers pulled at my throat.

"Relax. Breathe in."

"What?"

"I'm going to fill you with my breath. You breathe in as I breathe out, then we swop. It might make you lightheaded. Don't smash your head on the wall. It's a sort of vampiric breath transfusion. Should get rid of that confused haunted look which will undoubtedly ruin my picture. Don't argue. Breathe in."

God help me, I did. I inhaled him, coffee and wine and something slightly unclean, which made me retch when it hit the back of my throat. I gasped him down as he emptied his lungs into me, then, at a light touch of his fingers on the back of my head, began filling him with my own timorous breath. The air between us became foul. Sour milk and tooth rot. We sat together for about five minutes, mouth to mouth, not kissing, but panting into each other, harder and faster, until I could bear no more, and pushed him away.

"Lie down. Take some deep breaths. There's not a trace of oxygen left in you. You've gone very pale. It's a good look." I rolled on to the floor and watched as he grabbed his camera and started snapping.

"Tilt your head a little to the right. You've got quite a nice profile, actually. Bit more. Here –" and he grabbed my hair and yanked my face into the position he wanted. His feet wedged round my head as he squatted over me, clicking, fingers wound tightly, painfully, into my hair.

"God rot you," I said, then ruined it by giggling. His crotch was rather near my face, and spinning slightly. I could smell him, aroused and sweaty. I thought about making a grab for his cock, but it seemed too much effort, and besides, I felt I shouldn't distract him while he was being creative: on balance perhaps I would simply lie there staring at it. Quite meaty looking, or perhaps that was only the smell. I wondered if I might be sick, and if I were, if he would exhibit the resultant mess.

"I think that'll do. Stay there for a moment. I'll get you some water. You still look very pale. Pop your feet up." I did as I was told, and listened to his footsteps recede, the splash of a tap, then his noisy return. My mind felt completely empty, as if he'd sucked all my brains out alongside my breath.

"Here. Roll on to your right side and drink this. You've done very well. I think we'll get some fine images out of that. Did you enjoy being brutally violated? No need to answer. The camera saw everything. You have a very readable face, Clara, so don't trouble to lie. I imagine you'd come pretty hard now, although I haven't really time to experiment. You offer breath play, I see, so you know the effect it has. Face-sitting and such, I presume."

I nodded. "And choking, and drowning."

"Drowning! Fascinating. That is niche. Do you do waterboarding?"

"Sometimes."

"It's all about the spin, isn't it? The worst torture or the greatest pleasure, it's up to your brain to decide. If you're ever subject to torture – and from the look of you I suspect you are, daily – try to remember that. Find meaning in the suffering. Agreed? You can probably sit up now." He reached out to support my back as I swung into a seated position. I leaned against his chest. He was, I saw, unexpectedly hairy. I slipped a hand into his shirt and moved my fingers through the fuzzy curls. He allowed it for a moment, then lifted my fingers away and kissed them.

"Thank you so much for popping round, Clara. If you're feeling better perhaps you wouldn't mind – there's someone else coming at ten, you see. Sorry."

I shrugged to indicate my indifference to this news.

"I'll be in touch with regard to the exhibition, if you'd like to know how you've turned out. Good morning." He opened the door.

Chapter Seventeen

There are only two I can recall that I thought were proper weirdos, and I was right, but neither were dangerous. They were both so unforthcoming in their emails I thought it might be a police raid (is it illegal? Who knows? I am committing GBH, after all) or possibly a murder plot. It was neither. They were just a bit odd, but after a harmless fashion. One wanted to sit at his laptop looking at 1950s porn, chiefly pictures of women in corsets and those weird pointy bras, while I stood behind him and flicked his nipples with my fingernails. The other wanted me to read stories about spanking while he sat watching and recording me on his phone. For three hours. So, definitely unusual, but not dangerous. I've never felt the least threatened, and I must have seen close to a thousand people over the years. If I go to see someone new in a hotel or at their house, I have a safety buddy I phone in front of him, saying "I'm here and I'll call you in one hour when I'm done," like the escorts do, so he knows someone knows where I am, in case he's planning murder. Somehow I doubt anyone ever has been. Usually we exchange a whole heap of emails first so I get a good sense of them.

The worst problem I encounter is the no shows. I reckon at least 50% of newbies don't turn up. It's infuriating. I get it, they're nervous. It's a big thing to do, trust some mad woman you've never met to beat you in a way you hope you'll find arousing but might just find very unpleasant, but boys, I have to mark out three hours in my diary to drive to my mum's, get my stockings and make up on, unpack the canes, then do it all in reverse, so don't do it. Tell me you're not coming. Even if you make up an excuse. I've heard them all. Usually the car won't start, or they've really hurt their leg, or oh my God my dog's been hit by a car, would you believe it!! Well, no, I wouldn't. But I'm grateful for the heads up you're bottling it.

The no shows are the chief reason I no longer advertise. Plus all the emailing takes forever, and I've got a nice regular base of clients I adore. Some of them I've been seeing since the beginning. One told me he was dying of lung cancer about six months ago, and wanted to spend as much time with me as possible. He loves having his face slapped, but was struggling to breathe in our last few sessions. Slapping the face of a man who's visibly dying in front of you is an extraordinary feeling. I've not heard from him for a month or two, so I guess he's gone. He had a fantastic array of scurrilous anecdotes about assorted cabinet ministers and made me laugh a lot. I shall miss him.

Sometimes their wives know. More usually they sort of know but don't want to know, and operate a don't ask, don't tell policy. One chap was actually brought to me by his wife a couple of times, when she'd hurt her wrist and couldn't cane him herself. All kudos to her, although it was a bit weird for me, chatting to her about her health and grandkids while her fella ambled about with his not inconsiderable schlong flapping. Fun fact: most men can conspire to hide their bums for a week before their wives get suspicious, it seems, or at least, that's what men believe. Bottoms vary vastly as to how much punishment will disappear in a week, however. It depends on how practised it is at receiving, how warm you are, how much flesh is on your buttocks, any medication you're taking – a whole range of factors. The first time I'm faced with a bottom, I haven't a clue. I dread the newbies who turn up telling me their wives are away for a week and can I give them some cane strokes that won't last past Saturday? Well, no, I can't. I mean, maybe I can, but it would be pure luck. Best have a back up plan. I always recommend telling them, I missed you so badly I got maudlin and sodden drunk on whisky and fell down the stairs. They might not believe it, but you should at least get some credit for trying to spare their feelings.

The wives' feelings don't prick my conscience. Never have. Men won't stray if their wives give them what they need. Submissives are loyal, clever, desperate to please to serve, to have a Queen at the very centre of their existence, and if you're lucky enough to be married to one, you should jolly well get some stockings on and beat him when he needs it, or else not complain when he comes to me. I've never had a wife give me trouble, although I did have a daughter once email to tell me her dad was in hospital and I should "Leave him alone." He was the wrong side of Milton Keynes and inclined to grope, so I was happy to follow her advice. While usually I work at my mum's house, I also quite like travelling to people. I've been to Glasgow and Bristol and Norwich and pretty well everywhere in between. It's a chance to see the country. I've rented dungeons in London and Hastings and been to hotels and Airbnbs all over, taking care to book in my real name, especially with Airbnb – if they google my domme name I'll be chucked off for sure. Luckily my vanilla self is terribly dull.

I'm often asked if I switch. I will, very occasionally, if I know the chap well and trust him to be responsive and respectful. It's a huge privilege, because being spanked is important to me. Domming is an intellectual exercise, by and large; subbing involves my emotions and sexuality, so you need tread softly therein. Some of my clients are amazingly skilled at spanking, and some are just frankly useless, no matter how I try to instruct them: I still end up getting pats or brutally beaten, neither of which appeals. I've had my very best ideas whilst draped over someone's knee. Being spanked frees my mind to wander and reflect. That initial sharp shock of pain that fills your head and forces out all the worry, the rationality, the day-to-day tedious mundane chatter that's so deathly to creativity, then the steady pounding rhythm that forces you to relax and yield. Heaven. I love it and need it but it has to be done right.

But why am I telling you that? You know it already.

Chapter Eighteen

I walked five miles through fine rain that day. The pub irritated me. Richard's smug bitchy commentary irritated me. I had nowhere to be, just couldn't sit still. It's a common, cheap enough trick, leaving a girl dangling, anxious, then coming back to her with renewed enthusiasm: the relief feels something like love.

I'd been faithful, in my own way, always. Oh I'd lain down for the odd fella, of course, out of curiosity or spite, but I'd never felt any interest in them. This one, though. It was the silence circling intensity circling silence that was so addictive, but knowing that didn't help. You can understand the trick and still find the trick thrilling. It's all in the delivery and glitter, the sheer brazen chutzpah.

The exhibition was three days away. It was in the trendily ramshackle part of town, a former printing press ironically reimagined as a gallery. The kind of place I'd generally avoid, fear disguised as contempt. I never knew what to say about art. I'd taken Beth to see some stuff when she was young enough to be scooped up and have culture rammed down her poor wee neck. We'd walked round some good art and I tried to disguise how little it meant to me – Very nice. Lovely and blue, isn't? I like her dress, do you? – before gasping relief that she wanted to jump up and down the stairs en route to gift shop and cake.

Do artists really feel all that stuff? And if they do, why do they have to go on about it? It's downright vulgar to be so full of feeling some gets splashed on to a canvas.

Beth grew up to prefer maths, physics, solid stuff, not feelings, but I'd done my best. I barely saw her now. Passed her in the hall during her holidays, asked if everything was fine, meekly surrendered to her eye-rolling weary indifference. Occasionally she'd tut if I was in the bathroom when she needed it, and I'd accepted this was a close to communication as we now got. She'd taken to cooking up great vegetable and bean messes in the kitchen once I'd gone to bed, pulling every spice off the rack and leaving them sticky by the hob, so I knew she was eating, at least, probably better than me. I wished sometimes she might get some problem only I could solve, like the old days, when mum had all the answers and gave the best cuddles; I missed the thin plaintive cry that set breasts squirting. I didn't know if she had a boyfriend or a crush on anyone, or what telly she watched or her thoughts on God. She seemed stolidly content in her antipathy, and I had to be content with that. Sometimes I'd get home to find her and Rob chatting, but it stopped when they heard my approach, and I was too embarrassed to ask what they said when I wasn't there.

He hadn't written again since that last message, not a question, not even a suggestion of doubt, simply a command.

How is it possible to be so brimming with feeling and longing and have the people around you so utterly impervious to it? He was right: no one sees me. Thank God, in a way. But still. So lonely to face such a storm without a witness or confidante, family and friends oblivious. I can't tell. There's so little to tell, and what there is too shameful to describe. Is it love? It has the stink of love to it. The inability to think of anything else, from alarm clock cry to final, sleep-calling daydream. I want him to conquer me, humiliate me. I want to suffer sublimely for him. I had everything I ever wanted, husband, child, home, and having got them, it seems there's nothing left to want, save to be deprived of them. To chase this new thing, this fancy, balloon to a toddler.

If I thought he really wanted me it would help. It's the knowledge he doesn't seem to that's so tantalising. Everyone wants me, always. But this man, with his brazen indifference, his brusque bloody cheek, who doesn't seem to care whether he gets me or not – I want to master him, control him, force him to his bastard knees, and as soon as I've done it, I'll lose interest. I'll be fixed when he wants me. Then my want will evaporate like foam on the shore.

I'd reached the river and stopped to look at it, aware of how picturesque I must look, hair and coat billowing, moodily watching the water, thinking big thoughts, hoping passers-by would watch me and wonder about me. I wish I could just once inhabit my self without wondering what sort of impression I'm making to others. Rob's beloved aunt died and I held him as he sobbed and tried, really, tried, to be present for him in his grief, but at least half my brain was busy thinking: look at me. What a good wife I am. This is how good wives behave. No, more than half. I couldn't really feel anything for him at all. I was too preoccupied with thinking how I should respond to his grief in a way that would make me seem a good and useful person. Is that autism of sorts, or just the modern malaise? Style replacing content.

This man made me feel something. Disgust, fury, fear, mainly, and yet I'd started to imagine how our children might look, and yes, it had occurred to me I might be going insane. Bored shallow woman whom nobody sees. Why would they? There's nothing to see.

If I answered him the noise in my head might stop. It wasn't the fuck that worried me: that would be easy enough. Nor even the sure knowledge it meant nothing and would doubtless end with a solitary genital confab. It was the fear that the fuck might not fix me. That the feelings might not vanish.

Later that day I found myself hovering round the fridge, apparently hoping that sufficient cheese might fix my malaise, although no clear scientific evidence has ever confirmed the likelihood of this: then, after a half second of hesitation which I felt did me credit, reaching while simultaneously unscrewing a bottle of cheap white wine some punter had brought me weeks ago. I don't even like white wine. Beastly vinegary stuff, drying the tongue and hurting the head without a moment's intervening pleasure. Still, I chugged two-thirds of the bottle without bothering to find a glass, because I'm a proper hardcore masochist. Vilely sweet it was, too. I coughed, feeling the poisonous muck hit my knees, then my brain; staggered into the lounge, bottle still in hand, trying to think of something to do. Tidy up, that's it. I put down the bottle and picked up the faded petals from the carpet, shed from a week-old bunch of tulips Robert had brought home for me, all shy and pleased with himself. I pretended to be thrilled, but I bloody hate flowers. We chop them off in their prime, knowing full well it will kill them, which tells you all you need to know about humans; but also, they make such a sodding mess. Beth had left a load of cups and glasses and books on the table. I straightened them with a sort of passive aggressive mania, then decided I might as well do the washing up.

Now what?

I finished the bottle and reached for my phone, typed back, Fine, and wondered why I hadn't done that sooner, since I was clearly always going to do it: it would have saved me an abominable headache. I felt better, even when he sent me back a winky face, followed by one of those kissing lips emojis. Jesus, the man was a simpleton. This knowledge helped me too. I had solved the problem. You must get to breaking point, then break: it's really that simple.

I dressed carefully for my big seduction scene, of course I did. Stockings and suspenders, fuck-me heels, the lot. The knowledge I was going through this as a sort of parody of myself – chubby middle-aged housewife and mother breaks marriage vows with brutish simpleton – made it easier somehow. What the feminists never fail to fully comprehend: you can't be objectified if you've already objectified yourself, and you can't become a laughing stock if it was you that cracked the joke, then went on to point and hoot.

I hadn't thought much beyond his opening the door. He looked sweaty and anxious, shirt open a few buttons too many, exposing hairy chest and chunky, presumably ironic, medallion.

"Well," I said, slamming the door behind me, aware of neighbours' children congregating in the tiny playground opposite, the late afternoon sun exposing wrinkles and scars. "I suppose we kiss now."

He grabbed my wrists and pushed me against the wall, pushing his way into my mouth, rolling his tongue over and around mine. I stood there, impassive, letting him. Prisoners in solitary confinement would often slice or stab their own flesh, for the pleasure of feeling something again. I point this out without expecting or deserving sympathy; I thought the parallel might prove illuminating. His hands moved from my wrists, over my arms and made a grab for my throat, until, my face pinned in perfect position, he slapped it, hard, the crack in my ears hurting more than the actual blow. I realised there was a fair chance I might become one of those first date gone wrong murder statistics, which would be a horrid way for Robert to find out about my adulterous proclivities. Doubtless this fool would use the rough sex plea in court and the feminists wouldn't even bother to picket outside, because I'm a whore after all, and therefore a traitor to the sisterhood. I've spent my life making sure men get what they want, and women have hated me for it; if this is how my life ends, they'll all bloody cheer. The thought made me giggle. John frowned at me, looking genuinely furious, possibly murderous, which made me giggle again.

"Haven't you any wine? Shall we go upstairs?" I said, my whore training taking over. First wine, then upstairs. No, before anything you make sure you get the money first. Christ, I wasn't even getting paid for this. What the hell was wrong with me? Whatever it was, this fuck had to fix it, or kill me in the attempt. At least I could be certain now he wanted me. I'd stirred some feeling in him, seemingly, even if only an urge to violence. A connection, of sorts. It wasn't much, but I'd take it.

We only made it to his studio before we began kissing again. His honest hunger delighted me, like seeing a child devour the meal you've laboured over. We fucked on the floor, on his grey photographer's backdrop, which appealed to my inner exhibitionist. We were making a spectacle of ourselves, our own personal private arty opening, before the main event. There was a perfectly comfy sofa, but I realised it had to be the floor. This wasn't a cushioned, comfy sort of fuck, you see. Neither of us would get any kind of consolation from it. I distanced myself from the act by imagining what his camera would see. I would, at least, look comparatively thin next to his beefy thighs. His cock was circumcised, which made wanking tricky; disappointingly small, slightly pointy. I climbed on top to hide it from myself. He didn't like that, pushed me off, got me underneath; yanked my hair aside to bite my neck, hard.

"Don't!" I was too old to wear polo necks for weeks to hide ill-thought through love bites. He smiled, pressed his elbow into my windpipe, making me gag, then slapped me again.

It seems extraordinary, but my chief emotion was embarrassment. A sense of awkwardness. Where do you look, when you're fucking someone new? Into their eyes? Seemed a bit cringey, at least after several minutes of it, and he seemed to be having some trouble coming. I closed my eyes and moaned and thrashed around a bit, but that seemed cringey too. Eventually I settled for watching our copulation in the mirror above the fireplace, his big, hairy buttocks flapping and flailing on top of me. I stared into my own eyes, clenched my cunt and waited for it to stop. I'd read somewhere that sucking hard on your thumb makes your cunt tighten, mouth and gash being inextricably intertwined, physiologically speaking, presumably why so many sex-starved women get fat. He gave a small groan and pulled out of me to finish himself off on my face. Of course he did. That's what all the boys do now, isn't it? That instinctive impulse to reproduce bred out of our primitive brains by the preference of porn directors to zone in on the money shot, creamy spunk glistening pretty on artificially inflated, bulbous, painted lips. He pointed towards the bathroom; I filled the basin to the brim and immersed my face until I went dizzy. A baptism of spunk: a dunking in the ceremonial font after.

I emerged to spit the spunk from my mouth and blow it out of my nose, where somehow it had managed to wedge itself, acidic and sticky. His bathroom stank. Mould spattered the shower curtain. The threadbare towel with which I scraped away the last of him, rough and sour against my skin.

It was only afterwards I realised he hadn't said a word throughout.

Chapter Nineteen

So that's how a passing whim, a summer job, became my life. In Henry Mayhew's *London's Underworld*, first published in 1862, he interviews a former prostitute, now employed by a bawdy-house to look after prostitutes, and asks if she likes her mode of life. She replies: "I've been at this sort of work for six or seven years, and I suppose I'll die at it. I don't care if I do. It suits me. I'm good for nothing else." That resonated with me. I'm more bright than I am beautiful, always have been, but I've yet to find a way to monetise my brains: thus I choose to keep them for my own amusement, and flash my gash instead. Occasionally I feel angry and resentful that a woman with a couple of degrees can only get a decent living by spreading her legs. But I'm too old to change the world, if the world were even capable of changing. Instead I choose to adapt, chameleon-like, to my circumstances. I like money and attention and having a creative outlet, thinking up film scripts and erotic novels, acting, dressing up, being admired. These are all possibilities for me in this world and seemingly in no other. Occasionally I get a yen to become respectable, and then I start writing for literary journals or offering music therapy in residential homes or touring with theatre companies. It is useful having something to talk about at dinner parties. But actually, the closer I get to respectability, the tawdrier it seems. Musty-smelling, exhaustingly earnest, mucky round the edges. Seems the respectable people are beavering away trying to find what I've got already, money, status, job satisfaction, and wasting their damn time usually, certainly the working-class ones. That's capitalism. Gash sells, despite the fact 51% of the world has some. Luckily the other 49% wants it. I don't complain.

If you're a working-class woman who likes money, there's really only one path for you. And count yourself lucky: if you're a man in similar circumstances, you have to get into drugs, crime, things likely to kill you or send you to prison: at least my chosen path through the years won't do that. I could wish for different circumstances, but that way lies discontent, and not the divine kind. Happiness consists in wanting what you have. I've been a whore 25 years and I suppose I'll die of it. I don't care if I do. It suits me. I'm good for nothing else.

My friend the bawdy-house worker counsels loose women to invest while they're still in demand, and I followed her advice. I have a few properties now thanks to said magical gash, and enough income that I can stop whoring if I choose. Sometimes I wonder why I don't. But one must do something with one's allotted years, and all my friends are whores or punters, and they'd be upset and confused if I stopped. Anyway, it's a laugh. And when you come from abject, Dickensian levels of poverty it's really really hard to turn down money, even if you don't need it and don't know what to do with it. You remember how want feels, and you fear it more than death. The idea of turning down a wad of notes seems a crime of unparalleled magnitude.

I thought I'd write all this stuff to explain me to myself, and I think I've got me now. If you can't join them, beat them. Write that on my gravestone if you like.

But not yet.

Chapter Twenty

It was exactly 7 p.m. when I left his house. Gently closing the door I heard a church bell chime, like a call to prayer. Instead of which I headed straight for his stupid gallery, to worship at the altar of my own vanity. It was a clear, cold night. Stars were visible, if you cared for stars. I didn't. They had sod all to do with me. Men try to make sense and stories of everything they see, but it's all just about them, in truth, their own perspective of their story. I'm no poet. There were stars, so what? My feet hurt. I started to wonder whether after all my life mightn't be radically improved if I invested in more comfortable shoes, rather than chasing rancid strange dick about town.

I hadn't even said goodbye, just left. I assumed he'd want us to arrive separately. I wondered if he'd wash me from him, or keep my juices in situ, a glistening talisman. The last thing I wanted to do was go to some stupid posh art do with all his posh arty friends gawping at me. I didn't have the language or look to make them feel comfortable near me. My teeth were chattering. My breath steamed against the night air and I wondered how much of it had emanated from his lungs. My disloyal body had opened to receive a foreign object, closed about him like a wound, then continued to limp along without him. I wished there had been more violence. Something I could feel, sliced flesh, a bruise. A visible product of our coupling I could point to as proof. I pulled out a mirror to see if his toothy kissing had left a mark on my neck. It hadn't, but I still looked a wreck. Makeup melted, sex hair, pale. I sat on a wall to improve myself. There was a pub over the road but I realised I'd eaten nothing all day and this was no time to be seeking further alcoholic solace.

Under a streetlight I smoothed my face and hair into a shape more recognisably mine, although I still looked rather pale and angst-ridden. I would have to think of some way to get through tonight or not turn up at all. I considered how he had chosen me to photograph and me to fuck and presumably there would at least be some people at this exhibition of whom that wouldn't be true. But who knows? Maybe that's how he gathered a crowd. If I could feel only slightly special, in some way, if I could feel like I mattered, I could get through it.

But I went through it anyway, because I said I would and I'm a good girl that doesn't let people down even when they deserve it. I felt rather better for deciding to go through with it, the way the ill feel when they stop battling their ailments and surrender to feeling rotten and being bed-bound. The gallery was all exposed brick and thimbles of prosecco and gentle bell-like laughter and swirly skirts and chunky jewellery and very loud talk by people who knew exactly what to say and didn't give a damn who knew it. On a far wall, me. Splayed over a wall, hands crossed over my chest, bra straps pressed into my flesh, John's hand just visible, holding back my hair while I looked to the floor. I'd gathered quite a crowd. I wished I was staring straight back at them, defiantly holding their gaze, daring them to look harder. But I was looking away, wistful, pensive. People were murmuring about how it was interesting what he'd done. One woman said she wondered what I was thinking. I was standing right behind her. She could have asked. Although I don't know what I could have told her. What the hell was I thinking, then or now? For the first time I wished Robert was here to hear people talking about me, although he'd probably have hated it, and more reasonably, the urge that had driven me to it. My eyes had become the eyes, and they were being discussed. A knowing look in the eyes, they keep saying, and I looked, really looked, and saw what they meant. And an old weight lifted from my chest.

I found the prosecco table and toasted my triumph, literally raising a glass to my enormous image. The occasion seemed to demand it, but honestly I felt I would be drunk forever more on sheer pleasure. I watched the crowd mingle and swarm and felt myself a poet, a philosopher: every tiny detail resonated and throbbed with something new and magnificent, their histories and hopes glowing in technicolour before me. I had known happiness before, of course, when I'd managed to get myself knocked up, felt a wedge of notes stuffed sweaty into my garter, but this happiness had a purity and an intensity unlike any feeling I'd experienced before. This was happiness marred by neither hope nor fear; a restful, homely sensation. I walked through the exhibition, saw John in close conversation with a beautiful blonde, saw him and her and didn't see them, as if they might have been an indifferently drawn landscape placed in a shady corner. I padded through the place silently, occasionally turning to see myself, pausing and gazing, perfectly, permanently connected. No one recognised me. Why would they? The girl on the wall was me with my skin flayed free. But someone had seen me and acknowledged me. How desperately we all need to be understood. That's what I was thinking, although I realised it was John's thought, transferred to my brain alongside his rancid breath. How little sense suffering makes without someone on hand to witness it. Even Christ on the cross needed his crowd. Art is the hope of being understood. Beauty is as close to truth as most of us will ever get.

I moved out of the crowd, a newly formed crowd of myself, and walked away.

Chapter Twenty-One

"Have you got any of those disgusting sandwiches mouldering about your person? I think I might throw up if I drink more sans carbs. You know what, fuck it. Let's get chips."

Richard stared up at me, glassy eyed. "Still alive then."

"Regrettably, yes. I must have broken a mirror."

"How was it?"

"Boring. Stupid. Smelly. Yet weirdly liberating."

"How touching. Describe it."

"He was a shit shag and a decent photographer. He saw something in me I didn't want seeing, made some decent art from it while despising me."

"All artists despise their creations. Seeing him again?"

"Fuck no. No, I've got all I want out of that one, cheers."

He stared at me. "Poor silly soft child. I hope you've learned something useful. So what next?"

I sank down on the bench beside him, the ripped plastic covering poking into my flesh. Suddenly I felt terribly tired. I was aware of my makeup drying in my wrinkles, my ankles aching in their cheap shoes. I pulled out my laptop and opened my blog. It was largely mediocre, I could see that now, but there was something there, something I could use, and I could make it better, vibrant; real enough to hide behind. "Next. Dunno. Open to suggestions."

CPSIA information can be obtained
at www.ICGtesting.com
Printed in the USA
LVHW030711271021
701607LV00001B/5

9 781914 498138